**It would all be so simple for
someone to rob her right now.**

Gena switched on her turn signal, slid over into the exit lane,
and left the highway. Her eyes were glued to the rearview mirror. The BMW took the exit. Fear bordering on panic overtook her.

It's not supposed to be like this! Gena thought. *They must
know I got the money.*

She turned onto the access road and accelerated as hard as
she could. She would head back to Philly, where she could
lose whoever was following her in the tiny, narrow side streets
she knew like the back of her hand. She would run back to
safety and worry about stashing the dough later.

The black BMW sped up, trying to keep her in sight. Gena
raced down the access road. She could still see the halogen
lights of the BMW in her rearview mirror. And with each
passing mile, she became more of a wreck. She had her whole
life ahead of her, and she didn't want to die; not like this . . .

TERI WOODS

TRUE
TO THE
GAME
II

GC

GRAND CENTRAL
PUBLISHING

NEW YORK   BOSTON

Copyright © 2007 by Teri Woods
Excerpt from *True to the Game III* copyright © 2007 by Teri Woods

Grand Central Publishing
Hachette Book Group USA
237 Park Avenue
New York, NY 10017

Visit our Web site at www.HachetteBookGroupUSA.com.

Printed in the United States of America

First Edition: November 2007
10 9 8 7 6 5 4

Grand Central Publishing is a division of Hachette Book Group USA, Inc.
The Grand Central Publishing name and logo is a trademark of Hachette Book Group USA, Inc.

Library of Congress Cataloging-in-Publication Data

Woods, Teri.
    True to the game II / Teri Woods.—1st ed.
        p. cm.
    Summary: "The sequel to Woods's first novel True to the Game"—Provided by the publisher.
    ISBN-13: 978-0-446-58166-0 (trade pbk.)
    ISBN-10: 0-446-58166-6 (trade pbk.)
    1. African Americans—Fiction. 2. Drug dealers—Fiction. 3. Philadelphia (Pa.)—Fiction.
I. Title. II. Title: True to the game two.
    PS3573.O6427T78 2007
    813'.54—dc22

2007016555

I dedicate this book to my daughter, the most beautiful image of myself there could ever be, and to my baby boys, what a joy in my life, the greatest reinvention of myself. I love you all with everything I am. Always remember who you are.

—Mommy

ACKNOWLEDGMENTS

I would like to thank Hachette Book Group and Grand Central Publishing for the opportunity to be a part of something great. I am truly grateful to be signed to you. I would like to thank Karen Thomas, my editor, for believing in me and orchestrating my deal. I want to thank Linda Duggins, my publicist, for working so hard with me (you do have your hands full). I want to thank my publisher, Jamie Rabb, I love your style and I want to do numbers and I want to win! To Marc Gerald, my agent, who I always said would never be but I'm so glad you are. And to my publishing attorney, John Pelosi, you are simply the best. And last but not least, my life partner, Luke Riggins, for standing beside every step I take out here and for always wanting the best for me.

READY, SET, GO

The second time Gena saw the black BMW in her rearview mirror, she thought it a mere coincidence. The third time she saw the Beemer, she thought that it was just another car traveling east, among a plethora of other vehicles. And then she saw it a fourth time, and then a fifth. It was deliberately trying to keep its distance, trying not to be noticed, trying to blend in with the other vehicles on the highway. But she noticed it. And now she suspected that she was being followed. *Who the fuck is behind me?*

She stomped on the gas, only to see the BMW increase its speed. When she slowed down, it too slowed. And now she was about to conduct the ultimate test. She was about to exit the turnpike and turn back around toward Philly. If the BMW exited the highway, and turned around with her, then she would definitely have her answer.

Being followed was a frightening thing any day of the week, but being followed when you had millions of dollars in dope money in the trunk of your car was something else entirely. *Maybe someone seen me, maybe someone else knows.* Niggas had killed for less. And niggas had went hard in the paint to get paid. But this, this would be an easy come up for anybody. She had taken the treasure out of its safe hiding place, and now someone had painted a great big fucking X on her fucking forehead. It would be so simple for someone to rob her right now. She wondered if they even had instructions on how to do it. Peel back cap, dump bullets inside, take money, congratulations, now go live happily ever after, motherfucker.

Gena switched on her turn signal, slid over into the exit lane, and left the highway. Her eyes were glued to the rear-view mirror. The BMW took the exit. Fear bordering on panic overtook her.

It's not supposed to be like this! Gena thought. *Who the fuck is following me? They must know I got the money.* She hadn't asked for this. She didn't deserve to get fucked off, just because she claimed what was rightfully hers. Qua was her man. He was going to marry her, after all, and she was entitled to the money that he left behind. *I should have never took that keychain.* She had put up with a lot of bullshit for this money: bitches calling, bastard children, and hoes sweatin' her man all the time. *Yes, I shoulda took them keys, Quadir wanted me to have them, so he must have wanted me to have this money.* She had lost her best friend, she had lost her man, she had lost Lita. She had earned that fucking dough. And nobody had the right to take it from her. Not jackers, not the Feds, not the Philly PD, nobody. Fuck this.

Gena turned onto the access road and accelerated as hard as she could. She would head back to Philly, where she could lose this motherfucker in the tiny, narrow side streets she knew like the back of her hand. At worst, whoever it was behind her wouldn't be so stupid as to risk following her back to Gah Git's house. Niggas weren't trying to run up in Richard Allen and cause no static, especially at Gah Git's house. Gah Git was too well loved by everybody in the hood for that shit to happen. Naw, she would run back to safety and worry about stashing the dough later.

The black BMW accelerated hard, trying to keep Gena in sight. The driver didn't want to be detected but could tell he had been spotted by the way Gena was driving.

"Fuck!"

There was no doubt he had been spotted and there was no doubt that Gena was trying to lose him. The good thing was that the mouse was heading back to the mouse hole, and that was exactly where she needed to be. She would be easier to catch that way. And so would the money.

Gena raced down the access road, trying to get away from her pursuer. She could still see the halogen lights of the BMW in her rearview mirror. And with each passing mile, she became more of a wreck. She had her whole life ahead of her, and she didn't want to die; not like this.

A yellow light blinked on, and a soft chime rang out, causing Gena to look down at her dashboard. It was her fuel light. She had millions of dollars stuffed inside pillowcases in her trunk, and no gasoline in her tank. *Damn, I ain't never got no gas when I need it. What the fuck am I going to do now? Pull over, all alone, on the side of the road, with a gank of money in the trunk of my car, be robbed, or even worse, murdered. No, that bitch ain't me,* Gena thought, shaking her head. She was going to find a gas station. Maybe the motherfucker wouldn't risk popping her in front of so many witnesses; especially if she found a big gas station. An Exxon, Mobil, Valero, Shell, or even Lukoil; fuck it, we'll take Wal-Mart out this bitch! Just somewhere where there's a bunch of people around. She spotted the red, white, and blue Exxon sign just down the road, and a smile slowly spread across her face. She was going to make it.

Gena left the access road riding on nothing but fumes and raced into the gas station parking lot. The black BMW exited with her and followed her into the parking lot. Gena pulled up to a pump, while the Beemer pulled into a faraway corner and sat idling. The black sedan's dark-tinted windows prevented her from seeing who, or even how many, were inside the car. She climbed out of her Benz, hit her alarm so that her trunk would lock, and raced into the store.

"May I help you, ma'am?" the store clerk asked rudely.

Gena rubbed her sweating palms on her pants. "I . . . I . . . I . . . think that I'm . . . I don't know." She stuttered so bad, and her mind raced so fast, that she could not form a coherent sentence. "I . . . think. . . . Help me."

"What's the matter, pretty girl?" a voice asked from behind.

Gena turned in the direction from which the voice had come. She swallowed hard and shook her head.

When Jerrell saw her, he recognized her instantly. Although he didn't know her name, and he couldn't place her face, he knew that she looked familiar.

"What's the matter, ma?"

Gena shook her head. "I'm just . . . having a rough day, that's all."

Jerrell smiled at her. "Well, what can I do to make it better?"

Jerrell's smile was infectious. It made Gena crack a slight smile.

"There you go, pretty girl," Jerrell told her. "That's the way I want to see you looking. You feel better already, huh?"

Gena exhaled and peered out the glass window. "I think I had somebody following me."

Jerrell frowned, as thousands of thoughts raced through his head. *Why would someone follow this broad? She ain't even wearing no jewelry. Let me find out this bitch got a stash.* He would certainly stick around and find out. If not for some dough, then at least she would be a good fuck.

Jerrell clasped Gena's hand. "Show me who they are, ma. I'll take care a them niggas."

Gena was startled. The nigga was fine as hell, mad cute. But even beneath his good looks, a motherfucker could tell that he wasn't to be fucked with. *Thank God, I've been saved. This nigga look like he can go round for round, and he talks like he might have a little gangsta up in him. Yeah, he can handle this shit,* Gena told herself. And suddenly, she began to relax.

"It's that black car right there," she told him, feeling every bit a snitch.

Jerrell walked out of the store and peered in the direction that Gena had pointed. The black BMW was pulling out of the parking lot and turning back in the direction of the turnpike. Jerrell counted to ten, and then walked back into the store.

"Did you see it?" Gena asked nervously.

"I took care of them, ma," Jerrell told her. "You don't have to worry about them no more."

"Are you for real?" Gena asked.

Jerrell nodded.

"Thank you so much!" Gena told him. She wrapped her arms around him and gave him a hug. "I'm sorry, I don't even know your name. What's your name?"

"Jay," he told her. "My name's Jay."

Gena shook Jerrell's hand. "I can't repay you for this."

Jerrell nodded. "Yeah you can."

"How?" Gena asked, lifting an eyebrow.

"Let me pay for your gas, and let me walk you to your car and pump it for you." Jerrell told her. "And then let me follow you back to where you are going, so that I can make sure that you make it home safely."

Tears fell from Gena's eyes and she hugged him again. "I just met you, and you're so nice. I'm telling you I was really being followed."

"Hey, don't worry about nothing anymore, ma," Jerrell told her. "You're safe with me. I got you, okay?"

Gena nodded.

"Which car is yours?" Jerrell asked.

"The blue Mercedes," Gena told him.

Hot damn, that's what I'm talking about, Jerrell thought. *Let me find out this broad is rolling. No wonder she thinks she was being followed. Niggas was probably trying to jack the bitch for her ride. Probably a bunch of youngsters trying to make a quick come up. Jack her car, take it to a chop shop, make a few thousand. See, that's what's wrong with youngsters today; no fucking vision. Why yank the bitch from the car, and risk catching a carjacking case? All you got to do is just finesse these broads out here; stroke 'em, fuck 'em, and milk 'em until they credit card bills look like a New York lottery number. Youngsters these days have no finesse, no G in their game. But I'ma show 'em how it's done, baby; old-school style.*

Jerrell tossed a twenty-dollar bill onto the counter. "Put it on the blue Benz," he told the cashier.

Jerrell clasped Gena's hand and led her out to her car, where he sat her inside the vehicle and closed the door. Then he pumped her gas.

Inside the Benz, Gena closed her eyes and leaned her head back on the headrest. She felt something that she hadn't felt in a long time. She felt that she had someone looking out for her again. She felt like she had just met a really good man, one who wanted to take care of her and keep her safe. *Wouldn't that be something?* She missed that feeling. She missed being able to wrap her arms around a man and feel safe. She missed having the man of life in her life.

Jerrell finished pumping Gena's gas and then walked to the driver's side window, which she had rolled down.

"Hey, I want to call you tonight," Jerrell told her. "I want to make sure that you're okay."

Gena nodded, pulled a pen from her purse, and wrote her number on the corner of an envelope. She tore the number off the paper and handed it to Jerrell.

"I'ma follow you home to make sure that you're safe, okay?" Jerrell told her.

Gena smiled. "Thank you so much, Jay. You're the nicest guy that I've met in a long time."

"No problem, pretty girl," Jerrell told her. He caressed the side of her face, and then turned and headed for his vehicle, climbed inside, and waited for Gena to pull off. Jerrell pulled off just behind her and trailed her as she headed onto the turnpike, back to Gah Git's house, and back to safety.

His fucked-up crew had blown through all of his bread while he was locked up, and he had spent the remainder of his dough fighting that bullshit case. And now, now he had been given a beautiful, lonely, scared bitch to fuck. *Ain't life grand? And it'll be even grander if this bitch got a couple of dollars so I can come up again.*

"Woooooeeeee!" Jerrell let out an excited scream, as his imagination ran wild. He dreamed of fucking Gena on top of a pile of money, and then suffocating her in that same pile of Benjamins afterward. It was obvious that she didn't know who he was, and it was obvious that she was feeling all of the nice, concerned, protective shit that he was throwing her way. Which meant she was lonely and didn't have a man to turn to. *Maybe her man's in jail or maybe the nigga's just steppin' out on her every night. Either that or the nigga is a weak motherfucker and don't know how to protect his bitch. Either way, I got to find the story out on Ms. Gena.*

Jerrell had made up his mind and he had decided that he would get to work on that as soon as time permitted. But first, he had major important things to attend to; like catching up with all them niggas that fucked up his dough and had nothing but excuses about why he was broke. Yeah, he would take care of them, and he would get with his baby girl too. One thing at a time, though. One thing at a time.

"Don't worry, Boo," Jerrell said to Gena's taillights. "Daddy's here! Daddy's gonna spank that monkey real good, and give you all the man that you need!"

Jerrell settled in for a long drive back to North Philly, dreaming of what he was going to do to Gena and everybody who owed him. *I can't believe them niggas fucked up my money. They must've never thought I was coming back home.* Never once did he realize that the treasure he so deeply desired was only fifty feet away from him, in the trunk of Gena's car.

LET THE GAME BEGIN

Lieutenant Mark Ratzinger lifted his bottle of Advil liquid gel caps and tossed two of them into his mouth. He tossed the bottle back onto his desk and washed the pills down with a couple of sips from his coffee mug. He was up to about ten caplets a day. Those little green caplets, and his gallon of caffeine-laden coffee, were the only things that seemed to be sustaining him these days. Why, he didn't know.

He was divorced, twice, to be precise. With his last headache gone, he didn't know why he was so stressed out. Once the ink was dry on his divorce papers, he shouldn't have suffered from another headache, or at least that's what he thought. Getting rid of that bitch had been the best moment in his entire life, and to top it all off, he didn't have to give her a damn thing. She made twice as much as he did, and they had the good fortune to not have any little rugrats, so the divorce was quick, clean, and sterile. Kind of like his ex–psychotic whore, the one he called a wife, was in bed; quick, clean, and sterile. What kinda sick bitch cleans her pussy with an alcohol swab after making love to her husband? Yeah, he was real glad to be done with her.

Lieutenant Ratzinger rose from his desk and strolled down the hall of the busy police station and into a conference room where several occupants were waiting impatiently.

"Make your point, Lieutenant." Captain Holiday turned to him. "You're late, and some of us are very busy."

Lieutenant Ratzinger placed his stack of files on the table and walked to the blackboard, where he had photos of Philadelphia's various drug crews pinned up. Each group of photos was arranged in the shape of a pyramid, with the leader of the organization at the top. One group of photos, however, had two individual photos at the top of the pyramid. Quadir's photo sat just above that of Tyrik.

"This is our new plan, Captain," Lieutenant Ratzinger explained. "Working with United States District Attorney Paul Perachetti, we're initiating a new operation, one that not only targets the drug dealers, but aggressively targets their assets as well. We take away these assholes' money, we take away their ability to hire big-time drug lawyers, and to influence jurors and the outcome of their prosecution. We are going to hit them where it hurts, in their pockets."

"Not to mention, gentlemen, this department will receive 50 percent of the assets seized from these dealers," United States District Attorney Perachetti added. "And that, gentlemen, can add up rather quickly."

"And that's why the mayor is behind this thing, 100 percent," the deputy police chief chimed in. "A lot of nice shiny new equipment can be bought with this money, without costing the taxpayers a cent."

"With that said, may I turn your attention to the board, please," Lieutenant Ratzinger asked.

The meeting's participants focused their attention on him.

"Thank you," the lieutenant said. "On these charts are the organizational structures of some of Philly's most notorious drug crews. These pictures are photos of the main operators, or lieutenants, in these organizations. Up top is the captain, or head of the crew."

"Excuse me, Lieutenant," the deputy chief interrupted. "But why does that organization have two?"

The lieutenant turned toward Quadir's and Tyrik's photos. "Oh, because the one on top, Quadir Richards, is deceased. This organization is now headed by the gentleman in the second photo.

"Although Mr. Richards is no longer with us, his money still is," the lieutenant explained. "And we have reason to believe that this young lady is in possession of it."

"How much are we talking about?" the captain asked.

"Millions, we believe," Lieutenant Ratzinger explained. "Mr. Richards was one of Philadelphia's biggest and most profitable dealers, before his untimely demise."

"Who bumped him off?" the deputy chief asked, nonchalantly.

"We believe it was the members of a rival drug crew, known on the streets as the Junior Mafia," Perachetti explained. "I personally tried to prosecute the leader of the organization, Jerrell Jackson. Needless to say, I was unsuccessful. He walked away a free man. That's why I am really looking forward to overseeing the operation that Captain Holiday and Lieutenant Ratzinger here are putting together to get these scumbags off the street."

The deputy chief leaned forward in his seat and whispered to Ratzinger. "I want that money for this department and I want those assholes behind bars."

Detective Ratzinger nodded.

"See to it personally, lieutenant," the deputy chief told him.

Detective Ratzinger lifted a photo of Gena into the air for all to see. "This is a photo of Janel Scott, better known as Gena. She was the live-in concubine of Quadir Richards. And we are going after her, just like we're going after all the rest of them. We have to send a message to these young girls, letting them know that harboring drug money, and laundering it, is just as bad as getting out on the streets and selling the drugs themselves."

The deputy chief nodded. "Good, make an example out of her."

Lieutenant Ratzinger allowed a twisted grin to slowly spread across his face. "Oh, we will, trust me. We are already in the process of targeting Ms. Scott."

Khyree unlocked the door to his apartment and stepped inside. He carried with him two bags of groceries that he had just bought from the local store to replenish his nearly empty pantry. He strolled into his kitchen and clicked on the light, only to be surprised by an unexpected guest seated at the breakfast table.

"Jerrell!" Kyhree said nervously. "What the fuck are you doing here?"

"That's the greeting that I get?" Jerrell asked.

Kyhree set his bags of groceries down on the kitchen floor. "What's up, man? Good to see you!"

Jerrell stared at him in silence.

"Man, J, I'm so glad to see you outta that muthafuckin' place." Khyree told him. He walked to where Jerrell was seated and leaned over and embraced him. "That shit is for animals, man."

Jerrell sat silently, staring at Khyree coldly.

"Yeah, man, when we heard that you had won that bullshit case, we celebrated like a muthafucka!" Khyree continued.

"Where's my money, Khyree?" Jerrell asked.

"Money?"

"Yeah, my money?" Jerrell told him. "I left you with some work when I got caught up, and now that I'm out, I'm here to collect my money."

"Oh, yeah, the money," Khyree repeated. "Yeah, I ain't forgot aboutcha, baby. You know it's all good, J!"

"Okay then, where is it?" Jerrell asked.

"I got to get it for you," Khyree told him. "I don't keep no major bread like that in the house. I would have had it here, if I knew you was coming."

"Where is it?" Jerrell asked.

"It's at my other spot."

"Other spot?" Jerrell lifted an eyebrow. "What other spot you got, Khyree?"

Khyree smiled and exhaled. "Yo, J, why you tripping? This ya boy Khyree! You know me better than that!"

"The only thing that I know is that I warned you niggas what would happen if you fucked off my dough," Jerrell told him. "What? You muthafuckas didn't think that a nigga was ever coming home or something?"

"Naw, J, it's cool," Khyree told him, lifting his palms into the air. "Just calm down. I got ya bread."

"Then give me my fucking money, so that I can be on my way," Jerrell told him.

"Look, I'ma take you to the spot right now, and get you your bread so that you can quit tripping," Khyree told him. "I'm going to put this shit up, and then we can bounce. I just gotta stick this shit in the freezer so it won't melt while we gone."

Khyree lifted some frozen pizzas out of his grocery bag, opened his freezer, and placed them inside. He began to frantically rearrange the contents of his freezer.

"Looking for this?" Jerrell asked, holding up Khyree's still-cold nine-millimeter. "Nigga, I taught your muthafuckin' ass everything you know. You think that you can get me with some shit that I taught you?"

Khyree shook his head and let out an uneasy smile. "Man, J, it ain't even like that. I wasn't looking for that!" Khyree lied.

Jerrell set the gun down on the table and pulled another one from his pocket. "What about this one? What, are you going to sit down on the sofa next? Or go and use the bathroom? All of them are gone, Khyree. I got all of them."

Khyree began to bawl. "Man, J, you my boy, you know that! Why you tripping on me like this, man!"

"You muthafuckas fucked off my paper, Khyree!" Jerrell said angrily. "And now, I don't have a muthafuckin' thing to my name! Nigga, I'm scratching just to get by."

"J, I can give you some money!" Khyree told him. "Let me give you some money to get by with, and you give me a couple of days to make some moves, and everything will be all gravy, baby! I'll have the rest of what I owe you, and then some!"

"You talking about the money in that shoebox, nigga?" Jerrell asked, nodding toward a blue Nike shoebox under the table near his feet.

Khyree stared at the shoebox. "J, just take it. Take it all, man. I'll get you the rest later. Just give me a couple of days."

"A couple of days?" Jerrell asked.

"That's it," Khyree told him. "All I need is a couple of days."

"I got a better idea," Jerrell told him. "How about I take this money, and we call it even?"

Khyree nodded. "Whatever you want to do, J. But I swear, I can get the rest of the money."

Jerrell rose from the breakfast table. "Na, let's just call it even."

Jerrell lifted the black Glock and fired several times, striking a screaming Khyree several times in his chest.

Jerrell gathered up the shoebox and headed out of the apartment, stepping over Khyree's body on the way. "Now we even, muthafucka!"

MONEY AIN'T A THANG

Gena rolled over, clutching her pillow, as she opened her eyes to the sounds of Gah Git.

"Boy, if you don't come on here and put these pants on."

"No!" Khaleer took off running and sideswiped Gena as she was approaching the bathroom door.

"Boy," Gena said as Khaleer pushed by her and slammed the bathroom door behind him.

"Open the door." Gena tried the handle but it wouldn't turn. "Gah Git, Khaleer done locked himself in the bathroom."

"Gena, get me a belt. I'm gonna whoop the simple off his little black ass if he don't stop making me chase him."

"I'm gonna whoop the simple off his little black ass if he makes me stand out here and pee on myself. Gah Git, I got to pee."

"Me too," said Bria, who was trying to sleep but had been awakened by Khaleer's escapade and was peeking out of her room.

"Get me a credit card so I can open this door without breaking it down."

"I know that's right, Gah Git. Let me find out you be burglarizing the hood with secret credit card entries," said Bria, smiling at her grandmother.

"Go somewhere, gypsy child," Gah Git responded as she began to bang on the bathroom door.

Bang, bang, bang. "Come on, baby, open up the door for Gah Git. You know Gah Git loves you, baby, I ain't gonna hurt you, now come on, Khaleer."

There was no answer from behind the bathroom door. Gah Git took the credit card Gena handed her and opened the door to find Khaleer huddled in the corner of the tub.

"'Scuse me," Gena said, pushing Gah Git to the left as she hopped onto the toilet seat.

"When you gotta go, you gotta go," said Khaleer, showing a bright smile.

"Fool, you 'bout to go, go to ass whoopin' land, that's where I'm fittin' to send you. Now come on here and get dressed for school," said Gah Git, as she grabbed him by the arm and swung him out the tub.

"Gah Git, don't be mean," said Gena, pulling on the toilet tissue roll.

"Don't be mean? Gena, I been trying to get this boy dressed all morning. I'm tired and my day ain't even get started."

"Khaleer, why you won't get dressed?" Gena asked.

"Everybody teases me and calls me too short pants and they say the flood, it's a flood, and I'm not wearing them anymore."

"Boy, you gonna wear them, they clean clothes and you

gonna be glad you got them to wear. Ain't nothing wrong with these pants, they ain't even highwaters."

"Yes they is, Gah Git. I be wondering why you be putting them pants on him anyway," said Bria, teasing her grandmother.

"Didn't I already tell you to go somewhere, gypsy child?" she asked Bria before turning her attention back to Khaleer. "Now let's go, dammit! That's what's wrong with y'all now. Always worried about clothes and somebody else's name. Shit, black folks don't even know they own name but they know that Versace shit. Don't you know it's not what's on the outside, it's what's on the inside, Khaleer? You understand?"

"No, please, Gah Git, please don't make me wear them clothes," he begged before he started to cry as Gah Git dressed him in his highwaters anyway.

Gena sat on the toilet seat feeling bad for Khaleer. She remembered her school days and all the taunting and teasing she had endured. *Don't worry, cousin, I got you covered. I'll get you some new clothes today and won't nobody be teasing you when I'm done.* Yes, Gena had big plans for herself today. After finding a hidden treasure and safely hiding it, Gena had real big plans. She thought for a moment what she had done last night. *The money is safe; I don't have to worry about that.* Gena had it all figured. Last night after she met Jerrell at the Exxon station she let him follow her back to the city, but instead of going back to Richard Allen, she made a detour and went to Thirtieth Street Station. It cost little to nothing and was a brilliant plan. Inside the train station she purchased several travel bags. She went back out to the car and divided up the money in the pillowcases, placed it in the various duffel bags, then placed the duffel bags in different lockers. By the time she was done, she had eight locker keys. The nice thing was, she could pick the money up any time, day or night, move it elsewhere if she needed or keep it right there. No one would ever know what was in the lockers and no one would ever know she had found Quadir's money. *I got to get dressed. I got a lot going on. I wonder what I should wear?*

Gena looked at her closet. She didn't have much of a wardrobe to pick from. Actually, she didn't have anything. It had been like that for months. Gena sort of had no zest in her life, she had no romance, she had nothing going on that was exciting or adventurous, and for the past six months, she had done little to nothing except mourn the loss of Quadir. She didn't want any clothes because she had nowhere to go, but all that had changed. Everything had changed after she found that money. And what was even nicer was that guy she had met. She looked down at the piece of paper in her hand and wondered if should she call him. *No, not yet. But thank God for him.* If it hadn't been for him, she might not have been able to elude the BMW that had been following her. Because of Jay, she had been able to stash her cash in her secret hiding place without being followed. She kept only two of the pillowcases filled with money and had them in the closet, buried under her clothes, which were piled in even larger trash bags. *I hope Gah Git don't be snoopin' around in my room and find all this money. God, what would I do then? I can hear her now, boy oh boy, and I don't want to hear her at all.*

Gena carefully mapped out her day as she slipped into her clothes. "I sure do miss you," she said as she stared at a small picture of Quadir she kept on her nightstand. "Thank you so much for giving me the keys. I'm going shopping now, but I'll be back later. I love you." She kissed Quadir's picture and placed it back down on her nightstand. She grabbed her diamond Q key chain and headed downstairs.

"Gah Git, I'm gone, but I'll be back."

"Okay, baby, you just be safe out there. All these people with guns and stuff, they going crazy, don't make sense. You just watch yourself, Gena."

"Okay, bye."

Gena closed the door and looked down the street at her baby blue Mercedes. It was sparkling in the sunlight like a star from the twinkling sky.

"Yo, Gena, what's up?" the guy from the corner store called.

"Hey, what'choo up to this early in the morning?"

"Nothing, you know me, got to get a fresh start with this hustle shit I got going on."

"Well just be careful."

"I'm good, I'm on it. Tell Bria I'm trying to holler at her."

"Child, please, you better tell her yourself," Gena said as she closed her car door. *I got to get going, I got a lot of money and I got a lot of spending to do with it. I do not have time to be talking to you about your make-pretend love affair with my cousin.*

Her mind raced as she tried to figure out where to go first. She needed new clothes and new shoes and there it was. Sure as daylight was shining, there it was, the black BMW.

"Aww, hell no, not this following me shit again."

She turned on Thirteenth Street, then made a left on Wallace. *I can't believe this shit.* Yes, the BMW was definitely tailing her again, merely three cars behind her. *What the fuck should I do?* For thirty minutes Gena drove aimlessly, all the while being followed. She wasn't sure what to do or where to go. She wondered if she parked the car and walked on foot would she still be followed. Probably. She pulled into the Gallery Mall parking lot on Eleventh Street in Center City. It didn't seem as though the BMW followed her inside the parking lot, though. She kept driving up the ramp and then back down and then back up and she didn't see the BMW anywhere. *I wonder where it went?* she thought, still looking all around the parking lot. She parked her 300CE and paced herself as she walked into the mall, desperate to elude whoever was following her, but now that she was out of the car and in the mall, it seemed as if no one was behind her. If someone was, it would be hard to keep up with her. The mass of people shopping in the Gallery was her haven, a much-needed comfort zone. She walked through the lower level of the mall until she got to the Eighth Street exit, convinced she was getting away from her follower. She crossed Market and made her way over to Jewelers' Row, all the while making sure that no one was following her and there was no black BMW in sight.

She walked down Jewelers' Row looking at all the window displays until she came across a shop called Barsky's. She couldn't help herself, she just couldn't. When she found Quadir's safe, all she thought of was clothes, shoes, and jewelry. She wanted a necklace, some diamond earrings, and a bracelet, and the window display had the look she was looking for.

"How much for that?" Gena asked, pointing at a particularly brilliant platinum and diamond ring sitting in the display case.

"That one is thirty-two thousand dollars," said the jeweler, Ray Feldman, across the glass countertop case between them.

Gena nodded and continued to browse the items in the glass case. "What about this one?"

Ray lifted the ring into the air and quickly examined the tag attached to the ring's head. "This one is . . . twenty five thousand dollars."

"Can I see it?" Gena asked.

"Give me your hand," Ray said.

Gena held her hand over the counter, and Ray placed the ring on her finger. Gena placed her hand in front of one of the mirrors sitting on top of the counter and examined it.

"That one is my favorite," he told Gena. "I made that myself."

"Really, it is very nice," Gena said. She wiggled her finger, and the ring slid right off. "It's a little big, though."

"I can size anything to fit you perfectly," Ray said.

Gena handed the ring back to Ray, who wiped it clean and placed it back inside the display case. Gena pointed to another ring in the display.

"Wow, you certainly have good taste," he said with a smile. "I see that you dream big, just like me."

"I'm shopping, not dreaming."

Ray Feldman removed the ring from the display case and handed it to Gena.

"Well then, you're my kind of customer: sixteen thousand dollars."

Gena placed the ring on her finger. It fit perfectly, no sizing necessary. It was the one. If there was ever such a thing as The Ring of Life, this was it. It was a white gold ring, with diamonds embedded around the band, and a three-karat solitaire mounted on top. It shone in the light, like a sparkler on the Fourth of July.

"I'll take it," Gena told him.

Ray choked on his saliva.

"And how will you be paying for that?" he asked.

"Cash. Good ol' cash," Gena told him.

"That would certainly do, now won't it?"

Gena went into the bathroom and counted out sixteen thousand dollars. She handed the money to Ray and watched while he wrote up a receipt and an appraisal for her records. She walked out of the store feeling icy as she headed for another jewelry boutique.

"Can I see that watch right there?" Gena asked, pointing at a diamond bezel Cartier panther.

The salesman spied the ring on Gena's finger and immediately snapped to attention. "Yes, ma'am."

The display case flew open, and the salesman was snapping the watch around Gena's wrist before she could finish her sentence. The gold and diamond watch matched her ring to a tee. The only problem was that the watch and ring would both be on the same hand, leaving her other hand bare. She spied a nice diamond tennis bracelet that would help solve her dilemma.

"How much for that tennis bracelet?" she asked.

"Oh, that would look so lovely on you," the salesman gushed.

Gena caught the lisps in his words. He was just as sweet as apple juice.

"Let me put that on your wrist, honey!" he said.

Gena smiled and held out her wrist.

The salesman clasped the bracelet around Gena's wrist and maneuvered a large mirror in front of her. "You look simply divine."

She had to admit it, she was working those jewels. The only thing missing was something to go around her bare neck. She looked up to ask the salesman what he thought, only to find him rushing toward her with a necklace and charm. The boy could coordinate jewelry like a motherfucker. Yup, he was gay.

"By the way, my name is Carlos," the salesman told her.

"My name is Gena."

"Well, Ms. Gena," he whispered into her ear, "Mr. Carlos has something here that will knock your socks off. Close your eyes."

Gena closed her eyes. She could feel the necklace going around her neck, and the charm resting on her chest. It felt heavy. Carlos turned her around, in the direction of the mirror, perhaps. She would know in a second.

"Open your eyes, Ms. Gena," Carlos told her.

Gena opened her eyes and gasped. Carlos had placed a diamond chain around her neck, with a large, heart-shaped diamond pendant. The whole thing was breathtaking, and it left her speechless.

"You can wear it out," Carlos told her. "'Cause, girl, I know you will fight me if I try to take it off."

Gena laughed. This fool had to be the store's top salesperson. Her suspicions were confirmed when two fifty-something, super-rich-looking white women strolled into the store.

"Ms. Jennifer and Ms. Emily, I will be with you two young ladies in just a moment," Carlos told them. "You are rocking that new hairdo, Ms. Emily. You go, girl!"

The white women could not stop smiling, blushing, and gushing at Carlos.

"Now, Ms. Gena, how will we be paying today, Amex, Visa, Discover?"

Again, Gena smiled. Even if she hadn't originally planned on purchasing this many items, Carlos had sold her on them. His service and salesmanship were excellent, and he made her want to give him her money. She opened her purse.

"It'll be cash, Carlos," she told him. "I'm paying in cash."

"Girl, what is the secret!" Carlos blurted out. "I sell this beautiful jewelry to beautiful ladies like you all day long, and I can't figure out for the life of me what I am doing wrong! Carlos wants to shop here, too!"

Gena laughed, pulled out her money, and counted out the number on the register. She had managed to spend $130,000 in thirty minutes. She felt damned good.

And now, it was time to go back to the car. Gena drove a few blocks, observing that no one was behind her. *About time*, she thought to herself. *Or better yet, maybe it's about time that I get the fuck out of this 300CE and into something a little faster. Yeah, something new, something nobody will recognize, something fast as hell.* She headed out of the mall and to the Porsche dealership.

"Hello, is someone already helping you?" the saleswoman asked.

Gena shook her head.

"Okay, well then." The saleswoman extended her hand. "My name is Candace."

"Gena," she said, shaking the saleswoman's hand.

"What can I help you find today, Gena?" Candace asked.

"I need a car," Gena told her. "A really fast one."

Candace laughed. "Well, you've certainly come to the right place. Is that your 300CE out there?"

Gena nodded.

"How much do you owe on it?"

Gena shook her head. "Nothing, but I'm not trading it in. It was a gift from someone really special."

"Oh, well then, my next question is, have you ever driven a Porsche before?"

Gena shook her head again. "No."

"Well, we have several different models, and several different styles," Candace explained. "Are you looking for a convertible, a hardtop, or something in between?"

Gena lifted an eyebrow. "Something in between?"

"Yeah, like this, it's called a Targa. It has a removable roof panel, so that you can enjoy the open air. Not as much as in a convertible, but still, it's more than just having a sunroof."

Gena pointed across the showroom floor. "What about that one?"

"That one?" Candace laughed at her. "You want that one? That's a lot of car, sweetie."

"Is it fast?" Gena asked, not realizing the joke was on her.

"It's the fastest thing on the streets right now," Candace said in all seriousness.

A wide smile slowly spread across Gena's face. "I like it. That's the one that I want."

Candace placed her hand on her hip and shifted her weight to one side. "You want that car, right there?"

Gena nodded, walked across the showroom, and climbed into the car. Inside, she caressed the black leather diamond-stitched seating. Yeah, this was her shit.

"Gena, this is a convertible Porsche Gemballa," Candace explained. "It's a convertible 911 turbo. It's really a convertible race car, disguised as a street car. We're talking twin turbochargers, dry sump oil lubrication, Brembo Carbon fiber brakes, I mean . . . the works."

And it's black, too, Gena thought to herself, a rich, deep, shiny dark black convertible Porsche. It could outrace any car on the streets. And it even looked the part. The fenders were flared so wide, she could easily stand on them. And the massive whale tail and side intakes told everyone that this motherfucker could move, so get the fuck out of the way. Gena honked the horn, causing the other people in the showroom to jump. *Outta the way, mad bitch in a Porsche, coming through!*

Candace peered down at Gena. "Girl, what's on your mind?"

Gena smiled and shifted her glance toward Candace. "Can't nothing on the street catch it?"

Candace shook her head. "Nothing."

Gena glanced down at the speedometer, which stopped at 250 mph. "Yeah."

"Yeah, what?" Candace asked.

"I'll take it," Gena told her.

TAKE THAT

Paula opened the door to Gah Git's house using her key. She peeked into the family room. "Ma, it's me, Paula."

Gah Git peeked from out of the kitchen. "I'm here. Come on in."

Paula hurried into the house, closing the door behind her. She looked around her at the junky mess. *Why don't Mama make these kids clean up around here?* That was part of the problem; no one had to do anything. Gah Git did all the work, all the time. Paula was Gah Git's oldest daughter and was the most together sister in the family. She had traveled most of the world, had graduated from college, and had a master's in business. She worked for AT&T as a district field manager, which was how she was able to travel and see most of the world. Paula had worked hard to get to where she was and besides herself and Michael, her younger brother, no one else in the family had achieved as much success.

"Hi, Ma," she said, hugging her mother.

"Sshh, I got Malcolm on the phone."

"Who?"

"Malcolm."

"Malcolm?"

"Yeah, sshh," said Gah Git as she finished listening to her firstborn son.

Paula turned her back to her mother when she heard who she was on the phone talking to. *Malcolm, Malcolm, Malcolm, what does he want now?* Malcolm brought back a lot of pain, too much pain. Even though fifteen years had passed since he was sentenced, time hadn't changed the past for Paula. It seemed like only yesterday. But it wasn't for Malcolm; it was fifteen hard years served in a maximum state facility called Green in Pennsylvania.

"Okay, so September 12? Okay, I hope it works, baby. I'm gonna keep you in my prayers, Malcolm, you hear me?"

Paula looked over at her mother.

"Okay, I love you too, son, bye bye," said Gah Git as she hung up the phone.

"So, what's going on September 12, Mom?" asked Paula, being nosey.

"Malcolm says he goes in front of the parole board again. They might let him out this time. That sure would be something to see; my son, free, after all these years," said Gah Git as she started washing the dishes in the sink.

It be something, yes it would be something, hot damn. Please God, they had me locked up too long, even Maria forgive me. Sweet Maria, I'm sorry, baby, you know that, you know I am. I didn't mean to kill you, baby. I love you, Maria, to this day and all this time later, I'll never love no one but you. That's how sorry

I am, I just won't. I never meant to hurt you, I never meant to hurt you. God let me out of here, please.

"Scott!" shouted a correction officer on the block. "Scott!"

Malcolm was so preoccupied he hadn't even realized he was standing in the middle of a hallway.

"Let's go, keep it moving, time for count," the correction officer shouted at him.

Look at this guy, he thinks he's so in charge. Despite being locked up, Malcolm found a way to keep his mind free. But all those years were now gone from his life and he would never get them back. He would never get Maria back. He would never get the time back. There's a funny saying, *It's not what they give you, it's can you give it back,* and that is so much easier said than done. People don't understand what time can do to you, and then when you under the arm of crazy crackers and their bullshit, it can't get no worse. And escape, is you crazy? You not escaping, and even if you did, where would you go? In the middle of Redneckville? With nothing but mountains surrounding you and cascading along a never-ending skyline, where you going? And it seemed like the whole town in its entirety worked in the motherfucker. Shit was crazy. You'd have cousins, fathers, sons, and uncles all working in the same facility, all correctional officers. That's how all the prisons were in Pennsylvania. They were set up in those kinds of towns, with a bunch of rednecks, who now all had day jobs and benefits, and they couldn't spell *cat* to win a spelling bee. Can you imagine being nowhere, cut off from the world, cut off from everyone and everything that was your life? It had been the hardest fifteen years anyone could imagine, and to think of having to do another ten was pure D turmoil. *No, they gonna let me go. They gonna let me outta here this time. I just know it, I just do.* That's what got Malcolm through the day. The belief that one day he would be able to go home.

"Come on, let's go, in your cell, boy, get on."

Malcolm was already at his cell when the CO ordered him inside it. He just looked at the man, who was much younger than him. *You really don't want none of this, cracker.* Malcolm wanted so badly to check Mullinberry, but he didn't. Instead, he walked into his cell and faced Mullinberry as his cell door closed.

Let's see if you can count today, asshole, thought Malcolm as he lay on his bed and daydreamed about the upcoming hearing. *I know they're gonna let me go this time. I just know they're gonna let me go.* The thoughts consumed him.

"Mr. Scott, the board has approved your parole. You're free, Mr. Scott."

He couldn't believe it. He heard the words echoing through him as he looked around his cell.

"Are you ready, Mr. Scott?" asked CO Mullinberry with a kind smile on his face.

Malcolm picked up a photo that he kept inside a Bible his mother had given him. It was a picture of his daughter, Gena, when she was only three.

"I'm ready."

He got his belongings, signed out of the facility, and was on his way back home, back to the way things were, just like they were.

He got off the bus on Broad Street. Three blocks was nothing to walk. He pepped up his step as he passed by a small corner store.

"How much for those flowers?"

"Fi dahla," said the older lady of Asian-descent.

Malcolm walked out with flowers in his hand and made his way down the street. He walked into the high-rise tower and caught the elevator to the twenty-third floor. He unlocked the door and called out, but no one answered him. He heard a noise coming from down the hall. He set his flowers down on a side table next to the sofa.

"Gena? Maria?" he called out.

He walked backward, constantly looking all around him, keeping his eyes on the long narrow hallway staring in front of him. As he reached on top of a dining hutch, his hand felt the small metal .22 and his fingers gripped it. The .22 was a little something he kept in the house for that "just in case" moment in life, and he was starting to think that this was it. He moved down the hallway to his bedroom door. He pushed the door open slightly and peered into the candlelit room. It was Maria, his wife, his beautiful wife, her long hair, her long legs, her beautiful Spanish cocoa-colored skin, her voice.

"Ooh, papi," she breathed. "Yeah, papi, ooh," she said to her lover, who was holding her ankles up in the air.

It was then that out of the corner of his eye her lover saw the tall, dark figure standing by the door. "Ohh, damn!" he said, letting her ankles go and breaking the monotony of their rhythm.

"How could you?" Malcolm screamed as he attacked Maria's lover.

"Malcolm, stop!" Maria screamed as she stood on the bed as both men wrestled beneath her feet. "Malcolm, please, no, I can explain."

Pooooow!

The one shot of the gun seemed to echo throughout the room, and Malcolm looked at Maria's naked body as fear set over her face.

"What have you done? What have you done? Malcolm, look at what you've done."

He looked down at the bed, and with all the shock he had digested, his brother's face took him over the edge.

"You fucking my brother, my little brother?"

"Please, Malcolm, I can explain, I can explain," said Maria, pleading with him.

"I love you! Why would you do this to me?" He violently punched the wall.

"Malcolm, I love you too . . . It's just . . . we . . . I . . . Malcolm, please, I love you . . . I love you . . . too. I . . ."

Malcolm grabbed his wife around her neck. He threw her up against the wall. With one hand around her neck, he used his other hand to undo his zipper.

"Open your legs."

"Malcolm, no, Malcolm . . . please," said Maria, knowing that this was not Malcolm, this was an enraged man, and he wasn't thinking, his brother was lying dead and covered in blood on their bed.

"Malcolm, no, please," pleaded Maria, as Malcolm mechanically forced her against the wall and plugged into and began fucking her.

"Oh, God, Malcolm, no, please," said Maria, and the more she fought him, the more he forced her.

"You're a whore, you fuck my brother, right, you don't want to fuck me, Maria, you're gonna get fucked real good, you understand, you fuck me like him, you hear, I loved you, I love you and what do you do, you shame me," and with each word a deeper breath and a stronger grip, and as he came in her, her body went limp and he let her neck go, his grip crushing her windpipe and suffocating her.

"Daddy," called out Gena, holding the bouquet of flowers in her hand. "I have a picture for you, Daddy. See," said Gena reaching out her hand.

Malcolm quickly pulled up his pants and walked over to his daughter. He closed the door behind him and knelt down to Gena.

"Here," said Gena, passing him a picture, the same picture that now hung on the wall in his cell.

"Here," said Malcolm's cellmate, waking him. "Here's your mail, man."

Malcolm opened his eyes and looked at his cellmate. *Thank God he woke me,* he thought to himself, taking his mail. Malcolm hated that dream. It wasn't a dream, it was more of a flashback, so real, so like yesterday and so complicated. His life had never been the same after that. It certainly wasn't the same for his brother, Michael. Thank God he survived the gunshot, but Maria, sweet Maria died that day. Malcolm was charged with murder and sentenced to twenty-five years in prison. The only thing that saved him from a life sentence was the fact that he had acted in rage and the crime wasn't premeditated. In that regard he caught a break. But all that would change once he had this new parole hearing. His break would come. He knew it, he felt it.

Jordan's condo was located on the third floor of his building, overlooking a nearby state park. The views from his pad were some of the most beautiful and most breathtaking in the entire state. The condo had cost him a few hundred thousand, which he had his lawyer move for him so eyebrows wouldn't be raised and questions wouldn't be asked.

He had furnished the luxurious bachelor's pad with some of the most ultramodern furniture that could be found this side of the Atlantic. His caramel-colored round sectional had been imported from Sweden, while his metal entertainment center, metal coffee table, and metal end tables where shipped from Morocco. A stainless-steel Martin Bauer pool table sat in the middle of the room, just beneath an intricately de-signed, stainless-steel chandelier with Swarvoski crystals from Jay Strongwater. Soft, crème-colored recliners sat in front of a massive marble fireplace, while authentic paintings from Jacob Lawrence, Charles Bibbs, Sharon Wilson, and William Tolliver graced the condo's snow-white walls. A massive stainless-steel and glass dining-room table with overstuffed crème-colored leather chairs sat on the opposite side of the room. Beyond the dining-room table was the ultramodern kitchen, where stainless-steel Wolf and Sub-Zero appliances and crème-colored granite countertops could clearly be seen. The glass and stone sculptures throughout the condo screamed money, and lots of it. The game had clearly been good.

Jordan turned the knob and removed his key from the lock. He had been out shopping all day, and he was dead tired. He needed a shower, rest, and then he would hit the streets and pick up his money. And he had plenty of that to pick up. Business had been good.

The first time he heard the faint sounds of moving water, he had dismissed the thought as being ridiculous. Now that he heard it again, he knew that his ears were not deceiving him. There was definitely another person in his house.

He reached inside his gym bag and pulled out his nine-millimeter Beretta. He pulled back the slide, chambering a round, and then quickly ejected his clip and checked it. Yeah, it was full. He quickly slid the magazine back into his weapon and quietly crept over his marble floors into his bedroom. He couldn't believe that someone had the nerve to break into his crib. Of all the cribs in Philly, some stupid motherfucker had chosen his. Well, some stupid motherfucker was about to die.

The splashing sound of water told him that the asshole was in his bathroom. *You got to be kiddin' me.* And that was when he noticed the soft hum of the jets from his Jacuzzi whirring. *What the fuck! Somebody's bathing in my tub?* He just couldn't figure it out.

Jordan crept to his bathroom, shoved open the double doors, and quickly lifted his weapon.

"Jerrell!" Jordan cried out. His heart raced like a NASCAR driver around Charlotte Speedway. "What the fuck? Man, what the fuck are you doing here? I almost did you!"

Jerrell laughed and waved his arm, dismissing Jordan. Bubbles from the tub flew through the air. "Nigga, quit being paranoid."

"What the fuck are you doing in my crib?" Jordan asked. "What the fuck are you doing in my tub? How did you get in here?"

"Damn, thanks for all the love, partner," Jerrell told him. "I just figured that since we was homies and shit, you wouldn't mind if a dirty nigga like me washed a little bit a that jail filth off of my skin. I mean, seeing as how you got this great big old Jacuzzi tub and all."

"Yeah, well, my girl got a promotion," Jordan told him.

Jerrell smiled and nodded. "They moved her up from fries to milkshakes, huh?"

"Something like that."

"Well, why don't you join me in a toast, then." Jerrell lifted the bottle of Dom Perignon that he had next to the tub. "Go and get you a glass."

"I'm not thirsty," Jordan told him.

Jerrell shook his head. "Hmmmph, that's sad. Not going to toast to your girl's newfound success. What kind of a relationship you got?"

"We've already celebrated."

Jerrell nodded. "I'm sure you have, baby boy. I'm sure that you have."

Jerrell lifted his hand to his lips and blew some of the suds in the air. "You, Khyree, Mont, Ran, all y'all did a whole lot of celebrating while I was gone, huh."

"It's not what you think," Jordan told him.

"Oh, it's not?" Jerrell asked. "Tell me then, how much money did you send me while I was locked up?"

Jordan shook his head and looked away.

"Exactly," Jerrell told him. "You niggas was out here living large, buying new condos and shit. Everybody got new cars, new clothes, new jewelry, just everything, brand fucking new. But me, poor old Jerrell, I got to hustle in jail just to make a commissary on Tuesdays. What if I would have been desperate, J? What if I had to sell ass for cigarettes, or some shit like that?"

"C'mon, J, you know it ain't even like that," Jordan protested. "If you would have asked me, you know I would have looked out for you."

"Ask you? You had my connect, my spot, my runners, my

car, my guns, my ideas, my everything, and yet, I had to ask you?" Jerrell slid down further into the Jacuzzi, closed his eyes, and relaxed. "Okay, so I'm asking you now. Where's my money?"

"Is that what all of this is about?" Jordan asked. "Some money? You gonna break into my crib, jump up into my tub, drink up my champagne, and trip with me because of some money? Whatever happened to Junior Mafia? Whatever happened to us being family? What was all of that shit about us being family? What was all of that shit about us being brothers?"

"Are you your brother's keeper, Jordan?" Jerrell asked with a smile.

"You muthafuckin' right I am!" Jordan said forcefully.

"Then go and get the money that you kept for your brother," Jerrell told him.

"It's at the safe house, where I keep all of the dough," Jordan reassured him.

Jerrell laughed. "All you niggas got the dough somewhere else. The dough ain't never nowhere around, it's always a muthafuckin' drive away. You got fucking priceless-ass paintings and shit in this bitch, but no fucking dough. What, a thief a steal my hundred Gs but not your hundred-thousand-dollar painting? You got a muthafuckin' original Paul Goodnight over your fucking fireplace. That bitch had to cost a couple of meal tickets, but you're afraid to hold my chump change in this bitch?"

"So what are you saying, J?" Jordan asked.

"I'm saying that you muthafuckas are full a shit, that's what I'm saying!" Jerrell shouted. "The only reason I'm still in this muthafucka is to kill you."

Jordan smiled and lifted his pistol in the air, showing it to Jerrell.

"I think you forgot something."

"What's that?" Jerrell asked.

"I'm the muthafucka holding the pistol," Jordan told him.

"Glocks can shoot underwater," Jerrell told him, squeezing the trigger of his ten-millimeter Glock semiautomatic.

The bullet struck Jordan between his eyes, causing soap suds to mix with the blood that ran slowly down his nose as he fell silently to the ground. Jerrell climbed out of the Jacuzzi, wrapped a towel around his waist, and walked to the closet where he had Jordan's girl tied up. He opened the closet door.

"I know that I promised you that if you opened the safe and cooperated, I would let you live," Jerrell told her. "Well, the only problem is, I lied."

Tears flowed from Nina's eyes as she shook her head.

"I'll give you another chance to earn your life back," Jerrell told her. "You want to do that?"

Nina shook her head frantically.

"Let me wax that fat Latino ass of yours, and then we'll take a bath, and then we'll leave together, comprende?"

Nina shook her head.

Jerrell helped her out of the closet, led her over to the bed, and threw her down. He ripped off the buttons on her blue-jean skirt, yanked the skirt off her, and threw it to the floor. Next came her panties, which he quickly ripped off and discarded. He climbed on top of her and plunged into her, causing Nina to cry out.

Jerrell had not been with a woman since he had gotten out of jail, and he took all of his frustrations out on Nina. She bore the brunt of his anger with the Junior Mafia, his anger over losing his money, and his anger over having been locked up in the first place. He pummeled and twisted and gyrated and thrust like a demon possessed. He hammered at her as fast and as furiously and as deep as he could, causing her to scream and shout at the top of her lungs. He threw her legs over his shoulders and pounded as hard as he could. He had to get it out of him, he had to get all of the frustration, the anger, the fury out of his body. He had to exorcize the emotional demons that had become so pent up inside. He stroked forcefully, furiously, fanatically, until his release came. Nina could feel it shooting up into her stomach. She screamed, while he let out a deep, guttural growl.

Sweating heavily, Jerrell climbed off his victim, pulled her up by her wrist, and pushed her into the bathroom. She stepped over her boyfriend's dead body and began crying heavily.

Jerrell pointed toward the toilet. "Sit down and piss."

Nina seated herself on the toilet seat and urinated. Blood, semen, and urine poured out of her sore and aching vagina.

Jerrell pointed toward the bathtub. "Now, go and get in the tub and wash yourself good."

Nina rose from the toilet, pulled off all her remaining clothing, and climbed into the tub. Jerrell flushed the commode and tossed Nina a bar of soap and a face towel.

Nina began crying as she cleaned herself. "You're not going to let me live."

Jerrell smiled. "I have your money, I have your jewelry, I'm going to take all of your paintings and other valuable shit. I've fucked, I've eaten, I've killed the nigga that I came here to kill. What else is left for me, ma? Why would I let you live?"

"I won't tell anyone," Nina said, with tears pouring down her cheeks. "I'll leave town. I promise. I'll go back to Puerto Rico, even! I give you my word, I won't tell, I won't tell a soul!"

Before she could speak another word, Jerrell silenced her as he lifted his Glock.

"No, please, no!"

Those were her last three words before Jerrell fired one shot at Nina's head. The bullet penetrated her raised hand and entered her nose. She slid down into the bathwater with her eyes still open.

"I know you won't tell," Jerrell whispered. He turned and left the blood-filled bathroom.

HEAR NO EVIL, SPEAK NO EVIL

Reds wiped the sweat from his brow and slid down off the hood of his silver S500 Benz. It was hot on the block today, in more ways than one. The sun was beaming down on the curb, and the exhaust from the passing traffic only made things worse. But he had to be out there. His boys were grinding hard, and their packs were moving fast. He needed to be around to keep track of everything and to manage his young horses out beating the pavement. Today had been a good day so far, and it was only twelve-thirty. He still had the rest of the day left to get his weight up. His crew had moved half of the packs that he had brought to the trap, and the way things were moving, he would have to shoot to the crib and re-up soon.

"Damn, baby," Rasun said, wiping the sweat from his forehead. "Shit is rolling today!"

"I know," Reds agreed. "It's like the fiends all hit the lottery or something. It's fucked up to say, but crack is the best thing that ever happened to my life. I swear, thank you, God, thank you," he said, kissing a handful of money and holding it up to the sky.

Rasun walked to his candy orange '69 Dodge Charger, opened the door, and turned on his stereo system. The thunderous boom of the deep bass notes resounded throughout the area. Rasun had hooked the system up with eight eighteen-inch subwoofers, ten midrange speakers, and ten tweeters. A total of ten amplifiers helped to push out the system's awesome power. Rasun had the most powerful and best-known system in all of Philly.

"Pass me a beer," Reds shouted.

Rasun reached into his passenger seat, pulled a beer from the cooler, and tossed it to Reds. Reds caught the beer, popped the top, and turned it up, consuming fizz and all.

"Yo, you hear about that boy, Khyree?" Rasun asked.

Reds nodded. "Yo, that shit was ill. The boy got popped in his own joint."

"You think Rik had something to do with that shit?" Rasun asked.

Again Reds shrugged. "Who gives a fuck? He doing his thing, we doing ours."

"Damn, shit ain't been the same since Qua's been gone," Rasun said, shaking his head.

Neither of them, nor their crew members, noticed the two black vans making their way down the street. Reds looked up, only to peep the scene too late. *Fuck, I know that ain't ola.*

The Drug Enforcement Task Force leaped from the vans and raced toward Rasun and Reds. Other members of the task force leaped out of the delivery vans that had been parked across the street, while others raced from unmarked cars that had been in traffic. It had been a well-planned, well-coordinated raid. All of Reds's and Rasun's runners were gathered up within seconds. The task force had showed up in large numbers and they were all over the place before anyone knew what was going on. The task force moved like cockroaches when you turn the lights on. Everybody ran for cover like Olympic contenders. You never seen no niggas run so fast in your life. Reds turned the corner with Rasun following close behind. Reds hopped three steps to a front porch and started banging on the door of a girl he knew who lived on the block. She peeked out of the second-floor window.

"Why is you banging on my door like you crazy?"

"Let me in," screamed Reds.

"Boy, wait, *The Young and the Restless* is on," the girl shouted out the window.

"Bitch, open the door."

Just then Rasun peeped the task force rounding the corner and took off haul-assin', leaving Reds standing on the porch.

"Fuck," Reds uttered as he saw the uniformed enemy and took off behind Rasun. They made it no more than five hundred feet down the block before they were both thrown to the ground and handcuffed without being read their Miranda rights, as in most cases in the hood.

"Well, well, well, if it isn't Reds and Rasun," Lieutenant Ratzinger told them. "Ms. Clair is going to be real disappointed in you boys."

"Fuck outta here, muthafucka, talkin' 'bout my mom!" Rasun shouted.

"I just raided your mother's house. You know what I found, Rasun?" Lieutenant Ratzinger asked.

"You ain't find nothing," Rasun said, knowing that his

mom's house was clean. He began to twist and turn and try to get up. One of the officers put a foot on his back and shoved him back down onto the ground.

"That's right," Lieutenant Ratzinger told him. "We had your mother facedown on the ground in handcuffs, just like we got you. But she offered to give us some pussy if we let her go."

"You muthafuckas!" Rasun shouted. He tried to spit on the lieutenant, but it fell short.

"I went first," Ratzinger told him.

Rasun was foaming at the mouth. "I'll kill you, pig!"

"You can't threaten an officer," Lieutenant Ratzinger told him. "Especially one who's going to be your daddy."

"You muthafuckas make me sick. If I wasn't handcuffed I'd choke the fucking life out you muthafuckas!" Reds shouted.

The other officers piled the packs that they found onto the ground in front of Reds and Rasun. They had even managed to find Reds's stash spot behind the dumpster on the side of the cleaners that they were standing in front of, and Rasun's stash spot inside a box of laundry soap in the cleaners.

"Do you know how much time the Feds are going to give you for all of this crack?" the lieutenant asked.

"What crack?" Reds asked. "I don't know nothing about no crack. I was doing laundry, pig."

"Oh, a wise guy?" Ratzinger asked. He placed his shoe on the back of Reds's neck. "Let's see how smart you are, when you're sittin' in court, in front of an all-white jury, and I get up there and tell them how you said you wanted to sell drugs to all of the white kids you can find."

"Fuck you, pig. This the hood, ain't no fuckin' white kids around here!" Rasun told him.

Detective Ratzinger turned toward Rasun. "Tough words from a guy who just got his mom a federal sentence. Like it fucking matters; all that matter's is what the fuck I say."

"Leave my moms outta this shit! Ain't even nothing in my mom's house," Rasun shouted, speaking the truth.

Ratzinger turned to the other officers. "Get these two losers out of here."

The masked officers lifted Reds and Rasun off of the ground, walked them to one of the black, windowless vans, and threw them both into the back of it. About twenty minutes later Reds and Rasun felt the van moving, and within another hour they were at the precinct, fingerprinted, photographed, and thrown into separate holding cells.

It seemed like days, even though it had only been a matter of hours, before two uniformed officers unlocked Reds's holding cell and escorted him to an interrogation room. Reds entered the room and quickly noticed the large mirror hanging on the wall. He held up his right hand and gave the mirror his middle finger, knowing that there were detectives behind the glass watching his every move.

"Hey, listen, we're just here to help. So you don't have to be so negative."

"Fucking help? You not here to help. You muthafuckas never are," said Reds, wanting to spit in the officer's face.

"So, there's nothing I can get you?" asked the officer, again showing Reds pretend concern.

"How about a suitcase full of money from out the evidence room?"

"I can't do that, how 'bout something else?"

"How about you roll out the Blue Carpet for me so I can crip walk my black ass up outta here?" asked Reds, as if that would do the trick. "Oh, yeah, a Dutch and some chronic, too, while you at it."

"Hey, Bryant, let's get him something to drink," said Officer Friedling.

"Man, look, y'all ain't gotta bullshit me. I don't want nothing from you muthafuckas, nothing. So don't try doing me no favors. Unless y'all gonna give me my phone call so I can call my lawyer, I don't want shit," said Reds, being extremely confident in his choice of words.

"You haven't been given your phone call?" asked Officer Friedling, as if he couldn't believe it.

"Man, y'all muthafuckas ain't even read me my Miranda rights. I still don't know what the fuck you even got me in here for."

"No one read you your rights? Hey, Bryant, you hear this? No one read this guy his rights."

"Fucking read 'em for what, fuckin' niggas don't have any rights anyway, waste my fuckin' time reading you your fuckin' rights, fuck outta here," replied Officer Bryant, with a thick northern New Jersey accent, laughing at Reds.

"Man, fuck you!"

"That's exactly what they'll be doing to you, where you're going, hotcakes. Come on, let's get the fuck out of here," Officer Bryant said to his partner, Officer Friedling.

"Sorry, I tried to help," said Friedling, following behind Bryant.

Reds looked over at the mirror hanging on the wall. "Y'all muthafuckas gonna have to do better than that. Fuck outta here wit' your good cop, bad cop routine. Shit ain't gonna work here, crackers, shit ain't gonna work; fuck, fuckin' five-O, I hate you!"

Reds continued to sit there and grouse at the mirror, cursing, sometimes shouting, sometimes just simply talking, but saying nothing at all the plainclothes detectives wanted to hear.

Rasun peered around the windowless room nervously. He kept looking over at the mirror hanging on the wall. He knew he was being watched. He could feel the eyeballs eyeing his black ass as he sat there wondering when all this would be over. He wished this day had never happened. He sat still thinking of all the things that could have kept him from being arrested today. *Damn, I should have went over to my aunt's house with my mom like she asked me to.* Then he remembered what Lieutenant Ratzinger told him earlier. *Ain't no way they ran up in my mom's house. They must be bullshitting, yeah, they're definitely lying.* His leg shook uncontrollably, while sweat poured from his palms. His shirt was wet with perspiration around the underarms, and he fiddled with his fingers like there was no tomorrow. He knew the saying "never let them see you sweat," but he just couldn't help it.

The detectives watched from behind the mirrored-glass window, as Rasun looked as though he was about to explode.

"We can crack this cookie, look at him," said Ratzinger, watching Rasun's every move.

Lieutenant Ratzinger walked into the room with Rasun, closing the door behind himself.

"I don't want to talk to you," Rasun told him.

"Good, 'cause I don't want to talk to you either," Ratzinger told him. "The captain made me come in here to see if you wanted to work a deal."

"I ain't cutting no deal with you, so you might as well stop wasting your time," Rasun said.

"You know what, you're right."

Lieutenant Ratzinger picked himself up from the table he had been sitting at across from Rasun and walked out the room. *We'll see how you feel after twenty-four hours of sitting in that room with no food and nothing to drink.*

He walked into the room where Reds was sitting and found Reds still handcuffed.

"They still got the handcuffs on you, buddy."

Reds looked at Ratzinger like he was crazy. *Man, this dude is out of his fucking mind. Who the fuck is he calling buddy?*

Reds had decided he would have nothing else to say to anyone. They could send the president in this motherfucker, he wasn't saying shit.

"You know that's a lot of crack we found today, Reds. You guys really seem to have a very organized and profitable operation out there in those streets. I bet you make a lot of money. Hey, I understand, I know exactly how you feel. If I were in your shoes, I'd probably be doing the same thing. I mean, come on, let's keep it real. Isn't that what you guys say, keep it real? Well, I don't blame you, son. I just want you to know, I think it's a damn shame you're even here. You should be home right now. Hey, as a matter of fact, you should be hustling on your block getting money right now, and you know what, Reds, I'm here to let you go do that. I just need you to answer a few questions for me."

"Hey, buddy, let me keep it real with you," said Reds, leaning in to the lieutenant.

Ratzinger's heart skipped a beat and he leaned in to Reds

to hear what he had to say. "Yeah, let's keep it real," Ratzinger agreed.

"Suck my dick."

"Your choice, kid. You're going to jail."

He punched Reds so hard in his mouth that Reds fell backward in the chair and rolled onto the floor.

"Suck that, you piece of shit," Ratzinger said before walking out the door behind Friedling.

Two days had passed and they were still in the interrogation room. Unfortunately, Reds was requesting only food and blunts, and a television to watch BET. He would be a tough cookie to crack and he wasn't cooperating at all.

Rasun, on the other hand, wasn't doing that good. He wasn't as slick as Reds and wasn't as sophisticated in his answering techniques and he ended up holding conversations, and that was his first mistake. The police had him handcuffed, with his feet shackled. They escorted him down a long hall and into the back room of the processing unit. The police set up the stage for Rasun to see his mother being fingerprinted. The tears were dried on her face, but you could see her eyes were swollen and her heart was broken.

Ratzinger seated himself on the empty table just in front of Rasun.

"Here's the deal, Rasun. Your mother is going to be charged with the drugs that we found inside her house, and you're going to be charged with the drugs that we found at the cleaners. Things are going to get pretty bad for your family. Your mother is facing a very long sentence. She could end up serving a forty-year sentence at a women's federal prison. And let me tell you something about these women facilities. The lesbians outnumber the straight women, ten to one. And most of those bitches are built like linebackers from the Eagles. Your mother could end up doing some very rough time."

Rasun shook his head because he had completely forgotten that there was a quarter key of crack in the garage. He remembered hiding it there a couple of days ago because he didn't want to leave it outside in the car, just in case the car got broken into. He was supposed to relocate the cocaine, but he was moving so fast, he never took it to the stash house to have it broken down and vialed up. Not to mention, he was moving so fast, handling so much product, he forgot he had left that shit at his mom's altogether.

"Look, it doesn't have to be this way," Ratzinger told him. "There is a way to get your mom out of going to prison, without you having to take her time."

Rasun looked up.

Detective Ratzinger nodded. "And the best part about it is that you won't have to go to jail either. Your mom will be released, her arrest record will be cleared, and you'll be able to go free."

"How is that?" Rasun asked.

"Well, the way things work around here is that I look out for you, and you look out for me. We keep everything on the DL. It'll just be between us. I know that you're not a bad guy, Rasun. But what I need for you to do is to help me get the real bad guys off of the streets. You got a little brother, right?"

Rasun nodded.

"I want the streets to be safe for him," Ratzinger told him. "I want the streets to be safe for your mother, and your father, and your grandmother. We want them to be able to sit outside on their porch at night and not have to worry about some goddamn drug-related drive-by."

Rasun shook his head. "Man, I ain't down for no snitching."

"I ain't asking you to testify against anybody," Ratzinger assured him. "All I need is a little bit of information. Your man Rik, he's up right now. He took over the crew after Quadir Richards got killed, right?"

Rasun looked down.

"C'mon, Ra," Ratzinger smiled. "That is what they call you, isn't it? Ra? We already know most of the shit, we just want to confirm the shit that we already know. You ain't giving us nothing new."

Rasun shook his head.

"See, it's like this," Ratzinger continued. "Either you play ball, or we go all the way. We press full charges against your mom. And then, we seize your car, your mom's car, and your family's house. You know that we can do that, don't you? Since we found the drugs inside the house, that gives us the right to seize your parents' house. You want your mom in prison, and your dad and brother out on the street, all because you don't want to help us confirm some shit that we already know? Are you that stupid? Do you think that Rik would choose you over his mom? Do you think that Rik would let his mom go to prison for forty years, just to save your black ass? Rik's going to prison anyway. We're already on to him. We already have his number. Might as well save your ass, and your mother's ass, before we pick his ass up, and this once-in-a-lifetime chance goes away."

Rasun shook his head.

Ratzinger patted Rasun on his back. "I'll tell your mom that you said fuck her, Rik's more important."

Ratzinger rose from the table.

"Man, this is some bullshit!" Rasun said.

"I'm walking out of this fucking door," Ratzinger told him. "And when I do, the offer is off the table. If I walk out of this door, that's it. Your mom is going to prison, you are going to prison, and your mom's house is getting taken away. Every fucking thing that your parents worked for is gone! Gone! Do you fucking hear me, Ra? It's gone! All because you want to adhere to some bullshit street code that no one else adheres to anymore. There is no more code of omerta! There is no more code of silence! Even the goddamn mobsters sing like fucking opera singers once we get them behind bars. Well, you stick to your fucking code of the streets, and I hope you feel like a real big man, and a wonderful fucking son, kid! Your mother . . . Aw, fuck this!"

Ratzinger turned to walk out of the room.

"Okay!" Rasun told him. "Okay, I'll do it."

Ratzinger turned and smiled. He had figured that it would take more than one session to crack this cookie. These so-called street hustlers were getting weaker with each passing year. He turned back to Rasun.

"You made the right choice, kid. If it were my mother, I would have done the same thing. Fuck Rik. Your mother raised you, she's more important than that sorry, low-life motherfucker."

"You'll drop the charges against my mother?" Rasun asked.

Ratzinger placed his hand on Rasun's shoulder. "Kid, I'm a man of my word. Not only am I going to not press charges against your mother, but I'm not going to file the papers to seize her house. And I'm also going to suspend our case against you for right now. You do right by us, and your case will never go before a grand jury. You made the right choice, Ra. You chose freedom."

Ra looked down. He felt relieved. He didn't really fuck with Rik like that anymore, anyway. Fuck that nigga, he had to do what he had to do, that's all there was to it.

"I'm going to take care of the paperwork, and I'll be back in here to talk to you in a minute," Ratzinger told him. "I'll need you to sign some papers for me, and then I'm going to turn you loose."

"And Reds?"

"He ain't going to know shit," Ratzinger told him. "We'll run him before the magistrate, let him post bond, and then turn him loose too, that way you'll both be back out on the street and nobody will suspect anything. Trust me, we've been doing this for a very long time."

Rasun nodded. He had just jumped in bed with the devil.

SAY CHEESE

Gena rounded the corner in her brand-new Porsche Gemballa and hit the brakes. The BMW was sitting parked just in front of her. She couldn't see who was inside, and really, she didn't want to. She just wanted to get away from there immediately. And she did.

Gena mashed her foot down on the accelerator and the Porsche propelled itself forward like a fighter jet scrambling down a runway. The car's rapid acceleration thrust her back into the driver's seat and pinned her against it. She had never experienced power like that before, and she was glad to have it. The black BMW was nowhere to be seen.

Jerrell peered down at his brand-new Rollie and wondered where in the hell his date was. She was supposed to meet him at the park at six, and it was now five after. He wondered if she had stood him up, hoping desperately that she had not. He really wanted to tap that. Baby girl had an ass that you could set a cup on.

Gena rounded the corner in her new car and spotted Jay

standing next to the park bench. He looked fly, real fly. She could tell that the nigga had been shopping. Along with his fresh haircut, he had brand-new everything on. The sun was reflecting off his white Air Force Ones so brightly that they had to be fresh out of the box. The watch on his wrist and the piece hanging off his chain were sending off enough light to land a plane. She was glad that she had given him her number and even gladder that he had called. She pulled up next to him.

Jerrell rested his hand on the passenger door of the Guardsman black convertible.

"What in the hell are you doing with this?"

"You like it?" Gena asked, smiling from ear to ear. "It's my new ride."

"You mean, your man's new ride?" Jerrell asked.

Gena shook her head. "No, baby, this is all me."

"Yeah, right!" Jerrell laughed. "What happened to the Benz?"

"Nothing," Gena told him. "I wanted to park it for a while."

"Damn, so you balling like that, huh?" he asked with a smile.

Gena shook her head. "Not really. But I am starving. No, I'm famished."

"I was going to tell you to park your car and roll with me, but fuck that, I'm rollin' with you."

Jerrell opened the door and climbed into the passenger seat.

"So, where are we headed?" Gena asked, pulling off into traffic.

"Any place you want to go, ma," he said with a wide grin. "Tonight is your night."

"Oh, really?" Gena asked, lifting an eyebrow. "So, you going to spoil me tonight, huh?"

"The world is yours, ma," Jerrell told her. "The world is yours."

Jerrell turned and peered out of the window. She had bought a custom Porsche, easily worth over a hundred grand, and yet she claimed that she didn't have a man. *What is wrong with this picture?* Jerrell wondered. Her wrists, neck, and fingers were blinging more than his. He sat in the passenger seat adding up her wrist and fingers. *She holdin' more than me. Who the fuck is this broad?* Jerrell wondered. He needed more information. Hell, he needed a picture. And he knew just how to get one.

"Hey, I got a taste for something Italian, baby," he told her. "Let's go to the Spaghetti Warehouse."

Gena nodded. Spaghetti Warehouse was all right. Not too expensive, but pretty good. She shifted gears and turned the corner and headed in the direction of Spring Garden Street. *Could he be my new Man of Life? One never knows, does one?* she pondered as she smiled over to him.

"So, what do you do for a living?" Jerrell asked her.

"I'm kinda in between jobs right now," Gena told him.

Jerrell nodded, "Oh."

Maybe she sells real estate or maybe she's one of them ho's that sell cosmetics and shit. Naw, that shit don't pay. She don't look like a salesperson and besides the only kind of job she might have driving some shit like this is a lawyer or a doctor and she ain't neither.

"So what do you do when you're not in between jobs?" Jerrell asked.

Gena shook her head. "I just want to relax tonight. I don't want to talk about work."

Jerrell nodded.

Mmm hmm, she don't want to talk about work. I just bet she don't. She can't be in the game. I know all the majors in this town. So, who the fuck is she? A police bitch, maybe? Naw, she was too scared about being followed. Maybe she was pretending or maybe she's just fucking a real live nigga, either way it can only be one of the two. It's got to be one or the other. And I'm going to find out.

Jerrell crossed his arms, leaned back in the seat, and kicked the question of Gena's identity around in his head until they arrived at their destination.

The Spaghetti Warehouse was a quiet, romantic, authentic Italian restaurant nestled in downtown Philly. It was a casual place, with a bar to the left as you walked through the doors. Imported Italian travertine marble covered the floors. The restaurant resembled an old Tuscan village, with hand-plastered walls, Etruscan vases, stone columns, and wrought-iron artwork throughout. There was even an old-time trolley car that sat in the middle of the dining-room floor. Dim wall lighting was augmented by soft paper-covered candles on the dining tables. Modern Impressionist artwork graced the beige plaster-covered walls, while white-jacketed waiters and sommeliers fanned out throughout the restaurant, providing the guests with impeccable service. Gena and Jerrell were seated in the rear corner of the establishment, where they were assured their privacy.

"What may I get you to drink?" the waiter asked.

"A bottle of Pinot Grigio," Jerrell ordered.

"Very good, sir," the waiter told him, while writing down his order.

Gena closed her menu. "I already know what I want."

"Oh, then I guess we're ready to order," Jerrell told the waiter.

The waiter opened his tiny notepad again. "Very good. And what will you be having tonight, madam?"

"I want the chicken parmesan with a side order of fettucini alfredo and I think I'll start with a ceasar salad," Gena told him.

"And I'll take the same," Jerrell told him.

"And for dessert, madam?" the waiter asked.

Gena looked at Jerrell for a second, and then turned back to the waiter and shook her head. "We'll decide after dinner."

"Very well, madam." The waiter bowed slightly and headed off toward the kitchen.

"So, what do you do when you're not saving girls who are being followed?" Gena asked.

Jerrell smiled. "I thought that we weren't gonna talk about work. I was kinda looking forward to enjoying a stress-free, work-free evening, with a beautiful woman."

Gena blushed. "So what do you know about my restaurant?"

"What?" Jerrell asked. "You mean the Spaghetti Warehouse?"

Gena nodded.

"I eat here all the time." Jerrell told her. "The calzones are the bomb!"

Gena nodded emphatically. "I know! They stuff theirs with pepperoni and at least four different kinds of cheese! I love those things!"

Jerrell leaned back in his seat. "Wow! A woman who appreciates good food! You're a woman after my heart, ma!"

Gena laughed. "I love good food! Especially Italian!"

"So tell me this, Ms. Gena," Jerrell said. "How is it that a fine-ass woman like you don't have a man?"

Gena lowered her head for a moment and thought of Quadir. It still hurt deeply. She peered back up at Jerrell. "I don't know why. I guess I just don't."

Jerrell reached out and clasped her hand. He turned it over and examined her ring by the light of the candle. "That's some rock, ma. Big enough to choke a damn horse."

Gena laughed. She nodded toward the diamond-filled charm hanging at the end of his diamond-filled chain. "You're not doing too bad yourself."

Jerrell smiled. He peered up in time to see the restaurant girl with the camera passing nearby. He raised his hand and snapped his fingers loudly.

The camera girl turned in his direction.

"Yo, can we get our picture taken over here?" Jerrell asked.

The camera girl smiled and headed toward him.

"You want to get closer," she ordered, holding up her camera.

Jerrell scooted his chair next to Gena's and put his arm around her.

"Say cheese, baby girl," he told her.

Gena smiled for the camera, and the flash erupted.

"Another one," Jerrell ordered. He rose and walked to the other side of Gena, where he knelt next to her. "Get my good side this time."

Gena laughed, and the camera girl snapped the second photo.

The camera was a Polaroid, and the photos were instant. The camera girl set the pictures on the table, and Jerrell handed her a twenty-dollar bill.

"Keep the change," Jerrell told her. The camera girl smiled and headed for another table. Jerrell lifted the photos off the table and examined them. He now had two clear pictures of Gena, from two different directions. It had been the best twenty dollars that he had ever spent.

If Gena wanted to play Ms. Mysterious, that was fine with him. He had other ways of finding out what he wanted to know. He would pass the photos on to his man on the streets and have this bitch's entire history within a day. He would know every nigga that she fucked, all the way back to kindergarten, if she was giving it up back then. He would have birthdays, parents' names, brothers, sisters, cousins, and practically the entire family's history. He was Jerrell Motherfucking Jackson, and he didn't get where he was by not knowing how to dig up shit. This simple bitch was way out of her league, if she was thinking otherwise.

Jerrell lifted the bottle of Pinot from the table and poured some into each of their wineglasses. He handed Gena her glass and lifted his own into the air.

"To new friends, and to making new memories," he told her.

Gena clicked her glass against his. "To new memories."

New memories were something that she could desperately use. All of her old ones were too painful to bear. She had loved Quadir with all her heart. She had made that man her life. And now that he was gone, she knew that despite the pain in her heart, she had to move on. She had found another gentleman—another kind, sweet, protective gentleman—who was promising her a second chance. She couldn't believe it, but it was as if God was giving her a second Man of Life, because he had to take the first one away. She wanted this to work out. She wanted to be in love again. She wanted to share all that she had with someone again. She was convinced that Jay was the one to do it with.

Gena drank up, then lifted her glass into the air again. "To happiness, and laughter, and smiles. May they forever be a part of our lives."

"Hear, hear," Jerrell told her. "I couldn't have said it better myself."

Jerrell poured more wine into Gena's glass. He wanted her to drink up. He wanted her tongue to become loose. He wanted her to slip and say things that she normally would not say when she was sober. And even if that didn't happen, he really could care less. He would find out who she was soon enough. He would find out what she did for a living, where she was from, who her people were, and every damn thing else. Jerrell placed the photos beneath the candlelight once more and examined them briefly before tucking them safely away in his pocket. He didn't want to forget them, and he damn sure didn't want to lose them. They could be his ticket to a brand-new life. They could be his tickets to the jack of the century. They could be his winning lottery tickets.

WIRED

The van was disguised as a FedEx delivery truck, with all of the corporation's authentic logos, decals, emblems, and insignia. An officer disguised as a FedEx deliveryman even climbed out every once in a while and made actual FedEx deliveries to the businesses located on the block. Inside the van was a communications set without peer. The Philadelphia police department had spent millions of dollars on this super-high-tech observation post on wheels.

Detective Letoya Ellington sat at the communications console with her headphones on, listening as the van's digital recording equipment recorded everything that their wired confidential informant transmitted back to the van. They were getting some great information and had already gathered enough evidence to round up several of the smaller players who were engaged in the city's nefarious drug trade. But now they were gathering information on a big fish.

"So what price did that nigga Rik say that we can have them thangs for next week?" Rasun asked.

"The nigga said that he was going to give us a good deal," Reds answered. "If not, I hollered at that boy Blair the other day. That nigga got a new connect, and he says that he can help spread the wealth."

Inside the van, Detective Ellington took notes furiously. She was writing down all the names that Reds and Rasun were mentioning. The more Rasun talked, the more people they would be able to target for investigation. The more people they were able to target, the more people they would be able to gather evidence on. The more people they were able to gather evidence on, the more people they would be able to present to the grand jury for the issuance of indictments, and the more people they indicted, the greater the chances of convicting a larger number of scumbags. The more people they convicted, the better her chances were of making lieutenant. It was all a numbers game.

So far, Rasun had given them information on twenty-three people, and through his conversations with others, they now had the names of more than seventy-three drug dealers. They knew stash spots, meeting places, distribution locations, and even the names of some of the East Coast's biggest suppliers. They had names that the DEA only wished they knew about. Names that they would give the DEA to earn brownie points under the guise of intra-agency cooperation. Rasun had been a gold mine.

"So where's all of the shit that we copped yesterday?" Rasun asked.

"Man, all of that shit is at the spot," Reds answered. He was becoming annoyed with Rasun's constant questioning. "We gonna do this shit like we do it every week. I already called Ms. Shoog, and she said that she can cook that shit up for us tomorrow."

Rasun laughed and shook his head. "Old Ms. Shoog! She's gangsta, ain't she? Damn, how long has Shoog been cooking this shit up for us?"

Reds laughed. "Yeah, Ms, Shoog is something. That old lady think she got mad game, don't she?"

"She probably cook for half the niggas in Philly," Rasun said.

"That old lady probably been doing this shit her whole life. I know that she done cooked up more than a thousand keys for you. And probably about ten thousand keys for my nigga Qua!" added Reds.

Detective Ellington wrote down Ms. Shoog's name and typed it into her computer. A name, an address, and a criminal record popped up instantly. Ms. Shoog would have a nice fat indictment once this was all over.

"Sorry, grandma," Detective Ellington exhaled. "But, they got a place just for you. It's called a federal penetitiary."

This conspiracy case that they were building was definitely going to be picked up by the Feds. And if Ms. Shoog had cooked as much cocaine as had been alleged in the wire communications, she was going to go away for a real long time. So long, she'd probably spend the rest of her life in prison.

Rasun tossed Reds a beer and walked to his Benz, where he turned up the stereo system. He cut it up just enough to hear the music, but not enough for it to interfere with the wire that he had taped to his chest. He walked back to Reds's BMW and seated himself on the hood.

"So, Reds, on the real. What do you think the boy Rik is moving now?" Rasun asked.

Reds shrugged his shoulders. "Probably more than Qua was. Remember that nigga got his own shit, plus he got all of Quadir's shit."

"And that nigga don't even break bread with us like that. Nigga balling like that, you'd think we could get some better prices out of his tight ass."

Reds shrugged again. "You know Rik's ass is tighter than a KKK hanging rope. Just be happy that he ain't asked us about our side hustle that we got going on. I'm surprised that nigga ain't figure our shit out by now. I guess that nigga's getting all that money, he must be real preoccupied."

Rasun sipped at his beer, then peered over at Reds. "You think he know?"

Reds smacked his lips. "The nigga ain't stupid. He know that we done came up. He see the cars and shit."

Rasun nodded. "What you think that nigga Amin doing?"

Reds lifted an eyebrow. "Doing? Doing like what?"

"You think that nigga pushing more than us?" Rasun asked.

Reds shrugged. "How the fuck would I know? And why would I give a shit?"

Rasun nodded and sipped at his beer. "Anybody talked to Kenny?"

"Amar and Wiz went and visited that nigga the other day," Reds answered. "They got Kenny up CFCF still waiting on his trial. Man, they say that nigga's twisted in that joint."

"That's fucked up. You think he'll be all right?" Rasun asked.

"Kenny's not really the type of nigga that can do time. You know what I mean? He ain't built for that shit, you know?"

he asked, looking at Rasun, wondering if Rasun knew that he wasn't that type of nigga either.

"Yeah, I know what you mean. You think he needs some bread or something?"

"What nigga don't, but if the nigga done lost his fucking marbles like they saying, I wouldn't send too much at one time. Just enough, you know, to hold that nigga down for a quick commissary minute. I told y'all that nigga wasn't wrapped too tight. He never was."

"Damn, that shit's fucked up," Rasun said, lowering his head.

"I just hope that that nigga don't start talking," Reds told him.

"Talking?" Rasun quickly shifted his gaze to Reds. "What do you mean?"

"Talking . . . you know. I hope that fool don't start snitching and shit!" Reds told him.

"You think he would?" Rasun asked nervously.

Reds shook his head. "Man, you never know these days. Hell, the nigga right next to you could be in bed with them folks."

Rasun swallowed hard and took a long swig from his beer bottle.

Detective Dick Davis climbed into the back of the FedEx truck and removed his FedEx baseball cap.

"Whew, it's hotter than a witch's tit out there!" he declared.

Detective Ellington laughed and removed her headphones. She turned toward her colleague. "And you think it's better in here?"

"Hey, you don't have to carry packages up and down the street, sweetie," Detective Davis protested. "Any time you want to switch, you just let me know."

"Dick . . ."

"What?"

"Stop complaining like a little bitch," Detective Ellington told him.

The two detectives shared a laugh.

"So, are we getting anything good?" Detective Davis asked.

"Are you kidding me?" Detective Ellington replied with a smile. She lifted her notepad filled with names, dates, amounts, and various other information. "This kid's a gold mine! Christ, where the hell did we get him from?"

Detective Davis took the long yellow notepad and examined it. He smiled. "The kid's telling on everybody but his mother."

"Give him time," Detective Ellington replied. "He'll probably give her up too."

Again, the detectives shared a laugh.

"So, how are we looking?" Detective Davis asked. "I mean, as far as the grand jury is concerned?"

Detective Ellington shook her head. "Rock fucking solid. I just talked to the lieutenant. We're processing this shit tonight and getting as much as we can over to the grand jury tomorrow."

Detective Davis whistled, "Damn, that fast."

"Baby, we're trying to have the indictments out by tomorrow evening," Detective Ellington told him.

Detective Davis lifted an eyebrow. "Tomorrow evening?"

Detective Ellington nodded. "Tomorrow evening. It's

going down tomorrow. So, you can get ready for some over-time tomorrow night, baby."

Detective Davis tossed the notepad back onto the console. "The big roundup."

Detective Ellington nodded and placed the earphones back over her ears. "We are going to try to hit as many as we can at once."

Detective Davis whistled. "A lot of manpower."

Detective Ellington nodded. "We're going in with the Feds, the county, and just about everybody else. The Feds have some of the local guard on standby, just in case we need more manpower. I think they're Army."

Detective Davis wiped his sweaty brow and rose from his seat. He placed his FedEx baseball cap back on his head and grabbed some packages from the floor of the truck.

"Guess I better get back out there," he said, smiling at his fellow detective.

"Just another hour," Detective Ellington told him. "John and Rick are coming on duty posting as a utility repair crew. They'll be taking over surveillance then."

Detective Davis nodded. "I'll just be glad when this shit is over with."

Detective Ellington smiled and waved good-bye to her male partner. "Tomorrow, baby. Tomorrow, we'll be handing out indictments like Halloween candy."

"Trick or treat, motherfuckers!" Detective Davis said, laughing. He climbed out of the back of the FedEx truck and slammed the door behind him.

Tomorrow would be the big roundup. Tomorrow they would be taking a big chunk of Philadelphia's midlevel dealers off the streets. Tomorrow night, the jails would be full, and so would their evidence lockers, and the price of cocaine on the streets would be sky fucking high. But the best thing of all was that tomorrow they would be getting hundreds of dope-dealing sonsabitches off the streets.

GENA'S SAKE

Gena seated herself at the breakfast table and unfolded the newspaper.

"Any good sales in there?" Gah Git asked. She washed her coffee cup out and placed it in the dishwasher. "Child, I sure do appreciate this new dishwasher you bought me. I ain't never had nothing like this, all new and fancy. I can't believe this thing really cleans dishes."

Gena smiled and shook her head. "I'm glad you like it. I got some more stuff for you too."

"What?"

"Yeah, just wait, you'll see. I'm gonna take good care of you, don't you worry."

Gah Git exhaled, wiped her hands on her apron, and turned toward Gena. "Now, don't you go starting on me about no moving again. Girl, I done told you, I've lived here damn near my whole life. Ain't nothing wrong with living here. People just need to take care of they kids and work out they problems and be a family to one another. A few ass whoopin's and this place would be back to the way it was."

Gena laughed at her grandmother. "Gah Git, a few ass whoopin's ain't gonna solve nothing. Richard Allen is the worst project in Philly to have to live. At least let me get you a nice apartment in a decent neighborhood, since you won't let me buy you a house."

"Buy me a house?" Gah Git asked, placing her hand on her hip. "With what, Gena? Baby, you save your money. You done bought me enough already. A new refrigerator, a new stove, a new dishwasher, and all of those fancy new clothes that I ain't gonna never get to wear!"

"Yes you will. We got places to go and things to do. And for the life of me, why do you want us to have to live in these godforsaken projects? Gah Git, it's not safe, they always shooting at each other, and they killing people over here. I don't like it here no more. I used to feel safe, but now, it's changing. Ask Gary, he's in the streets, he'll tell you the same thing," Gena said, trying to convince her grandmother of the truth.

"Look, Gena, I'm used to it. I done lived here all my life. I don't want to go, that's all. Now leave me alone."

"Man, Gah Git, I don't even sleep with all the sirens and guns poppin' off, and I'm scared to walk to the store. See, you always sending us. But that's not right. You go on out there and see if you like walking down the street. Shoot, I bet you'll be ready to move then."

"Now, Gena, you can't be scared of your own people, baby," Gah Git told her. "You can't never do that, you hear me? That's what got us into this predicament in the first place. Black folks not trusting other black folks and we separated. You hear me?"

"Gah Git, black folks can't trust black folks 'cause white folks got all the money. If black folks had all the money like white folks, there wouldn't be no issues and black folks would be all right."

"This may be true, but the white man ain't giving up nothing, so black folks need to stick together. You youngins sure got a long hard road to travel."

"Yes, ma'am, that road is mighty rough too," Gena joked. "But still why we got to be in Rich—"

"Ain't no but still," Gah Git said, dismissing her with a wave of her hand. "I'm gon' stay right here, right here where I'm at. I don't even know why I'm wastin' time talking this long. This is where I raised all my kids, Gena, and all my grandkids; it's what I know. Shoot, I done raised a whole lot of other folks' kids. Gah Git is just fine, right where she is."

Gena exhaled and shook her head.

Gah Git turned back toward the sink, where her dishwasher was waiting for her.

"Gena, don't you go and get no big head now, just 'cause you done got a good job and all."

"I'm not, Gah Git," Gena protested. "It's just that I'm worried about you."

"What are you worried about me for?" Gah Git asked. "You thinking about getting outta here and moving in with that new boyfriend a yours? Don'tcha do it. Don't you even think about it. Every time you date a man, you got to go live with 'em. I don't understand it."

"No, no, I'm not ever doing that no more. Besides, I don't want to live with Jay. Dag, I remember when Jamal threw me out and had my clothes all in the street. Gah Git, it was a mess. You just don't know what I go through, and then Quadir, with that house we had . . ." And she stopped and looked off to the side. "But I am thinking about getting something somewhere nice. I just wish you would come with me."

"All right now, sugar pie, that's what I'm talking about, girl. God bless the child that got his own," Gah Git said, scrubbing dishes and placing them into the dishwasher. "Didn't I tell you a man will never buy the cow if he can get the milk for free?"

"Uh, yeah, I think you have," said Gena, laughing at Gah Git, who was just as serious as serious could be. Gah Git had told her that line a million times now. "Hey, Gah Git, ain't no milking going on here."

"'Bout time, 'cause I sure do hope so, 'cause them gypsy-ass cousins of yours is gone," Gah Git turned toward her. "You should talk to 'em."

Gena lifted an eyebrow. "Who? Brianna and Bria? You think that they're sexually active, Gah Git?"

"Sexually active?" Gah Git placed the bowl that she was washing into the dishwasher and then placed her hand on her hip. "Girl, sexually active ain't the word. Them girls is passing out tail like it's government cheese."

Gena spat out her milk.

"Gah Git!"

"What? You think I don't know what's going on around here?" Gah Git asked.

Wow, Gena couldn't help but to think to herself. She really wasn't minding them like that, dealing with the loss of Quadir and moving back home. Gena shook her head. "No,

I know that you know everything that's going on within a fifty-block radius. But still . . ."

"But still, nothing, you should try to talk to them about it, because they keep telling me I'm too old and I don't understand. Brianna told me, 'Oh, Gah Git, it's just sex.' They not giving me no heart attack. So, I done told them girls not to be messing around and if that's what they gonna do, then God help 'em and use a condom and protect they self. They said I'm too old to know. I know more than them." Gah Git turned back toward her dishes. She didn't want to talk about them no more. Bria and Brianna had hurt her feelings, but more important, the young girls shut her out because she was older, not knowing that Gah Git had answers to help guide them. But Gah Git couldn't talk to them, just couldn't reach them.

"So, what's the deal with this new man, and when can I meet him?"

"Meet him?" Gena asked, surprised. "You want to meet him?"

"I want to meet the man who got you out of your frumpy frowning ways," Gah Git told her. "Baby, it's good to see you smiling again. It's so good to see you living again," she said gently, holding Gena's cheeks in her hands. "I know that you loved Quadir, but he's gone now. And he would want you to be happy."

Gena smiled and lowered her head. She didn't know if she was ready to have this conversation with Gah Git. She still wasn't sure if she was ready to begin letting go.

"We still here, baby," Gah Git continued. "And we got to keep on living and keep on loving. We got to live life for those we love. We got to do things that they can't do no more. We got to live life for them too.

"You know I need to talk to you about something." Gah Git wiped her hands on her apron, stopped what she was doing, and sat down at the table with Gena.

"Why you looking so serious?" Gena asked, smiling at her grandmother.

Gah Git didn't know where to begin. She didn't know where to start. How do you tell somebody that her father might not be her father? She picked up a napkin and began ruffling it through her fingers, and just when she was about to begin, Bria stormed into the house, letting Gena's cat, Gucci, in with her.

Gah Git quickly stood up from the table. "Mmm-mmm, I'm not sure what to say out my mouth; if it ain't Ms. Five O'clock in the Morning! You came up in this house at five o'clock in the morning and somehow you got out of here before I could get a hold of you this morning. You know damn well that you supposed to have your butt in this house by ten o'clock at night! Where was you at?"

"Please, Gah Git, please don't ask me questions like that. I was over Dalvin's house and I fell asleep. What's the big deal?" Bria responded as she waved her hand in the air at her grandmother.

"Who you think you talking to like that?" asked Gah Git as she wiped her hands on her apron, ready to smack the shit out of Bria. "Young lady, we have rules in this house. And you will obey those rules."

"Fuck rules," Bria whispered under her breath as she huffed herself upstairs.

"Excuse me?" Gena asked. "What did you just say?"

"I wasn't even talking to you," Bria told her. "So mind your business."

"You are so disrespectful. It is my business if you disrespecting Gah Git!" Gena snapped back.

"No, it ain't none a yo business if I'm not talking to you!" Bria shouted, shaking her head. "You ain't my mama, Gena! And you need to stop acting like it!"

"I know that I ain't your mama, your mama is on crack right now, that's why you live here. So, you need to show some respect."

"Whatever, your mama's dead, 'cause your daddy killed her, now!" said Bria, rolling her eyes at Gena and continuing upstairs.

"Bria!" yelled Gah Git. "What the hell is wrong with you; come back down here, come back down here right now, 'cause if I got to come up them steps to get you, so help me God, I might hurt you, girl."

As she walked back down the stairs, Bria thought about what she had said, and in her heart of hearts she knew she had crossed the line. Even if she and Gena never did get along, that was still no reason for her to say what she had just said. She didn't realize it, but Bria had just unleashed the biggest family secret, and Gah Git had reached her boiling point. She slapped Bria across the face harder than she's ever hit anything in her life, spinning Bria around and knocking her into the wall before she fell to the floor.

Bria looked up at her grandmother and then over to Gena, who seemed to not have heard her.

"What did you say?" asked Gena, looking confused.

"Nothing, baby, she ain't say nothing. Bria, go upstairs in

your room and you stay there until I tell you different, you hear me?" Gah Git asked her, squeezing her arm.

"Mmm hmm."

"I can't hear you, what you say?" asked Gah Git, squeezing her arm harder.

"Yes, ma'am."

"That's what I thought you said. I wasn't sure, I just had to make sure I was hearing you," said Gah Git, still squeezing her arm as she led Bria over to the staircase.

"I'll deal with you later. You hear me, I'ma deal with you, though. You got some nerve, honey, some nerve. But I will deal with you if it kills me, you gonna learn to respect me and this house."

Just then Brianna flung open the door and walked in from school.

"Dag, what's going on in here?" Brianna asked.

Gah Git didn't know what to say. She looked at Gena, who seemed confused and unsure of what she had just heard.

"Gena, you all right?" asked Brianna before hugging her grandmother.

"Yeah, she all right, now go on upstairs for me and give me a few minutes with your cousin," said Gah Git, pushing Brianna over to the staircase.

"Okay, wait . . . hold up, Gah Git, can I just get some juice?" asked Brianna, who was trying to avoid being pushed away.

"No! Juice ain't no good for you, it's loaded with sugar. Just go on upstairs like I said now."

"Dag, okay, let me get my book bag, Gah Git," said Brianna, as Gah Git continued to push her.

"Gah Git, okay, I'm going on upstairs. You squeezing my

arm, Gah Git, I didn't even do nothing," said Brianna, trying to get free. "Dag, Gah Git, why you hurting me? I didn't do nothing," she added, not wanting to go upstairs but running out of reasons to procrastinate.

Brianna folded her arms and smacked her lips at Gah Git.

"Okay, I'll see y'all later, since I'm being forced to go upstairs."

"Bye, good riddance, go!" said Gah Git. She turned and walked over to Gena. "Hey, see, I was trying to talk to you, but Bria came in and I forgot what I was about to say," said Gah Git, not sure what to say.

"I got to go," said Gena, looking as if she had just been hit by a softball in the back of the head. She ran upstairs to her room and began to pack a carrying bag.

"Go where?" said Gah Git, following Gena through the house, standing in her doorway.

"I don't know, Gah Git, just away from here. Just to myself, please let me be."

"Awww, baby, don't be that way. You know I love you."

"Love has nothing to do with my mother not being here."

Gena looked at her grandmother with eyes of ice. Gah Git said no more after she gave her that look, and silence grew thick in the air as she stood back and watched Gena rush past her and down the stairs. She heard the front door slam closed and she knew that she should have told Gena the truth a long time ago. She had raised Gena to live a lie. Even though it was a lie to protect her, all in all, it was still a lie. She walked into her room and sat on the edge of her bed. Gah Git looked over to her tabletop at the various pictures of her children and her husband. So many memories. Some were good and some were bad. She picked up the phone and dialed her youngest son, Michael. It was time, time to tell the truth, and time for Michael to come back home. She would have him come home right away, if for nothing else, for the sake of Gena.

ANOTHER DAY IN THE TRENCHES

Mont rode his Suzuki GSXR 1300 Hayabusa to his brother's bike shop. The bike was brand new to the market, and not many of them were out on the streets yet. It was the latest toy, his pride and joy, and he had already spent more than fifteen thousand dollars in modifications on it.

The Hayabusa had been painted money green, with hundred-dollar bills painted all over the bike. The frame had been chromed, as had all of the bike's other metal parts. The bike had been modified with a rear extended swing arm that had been chromed out, along with a rear fat boy rim and tire. The bike's engine had been juiced up with a newly installed power commander, a Garrett turbocharger, and nitros system. It was, without a doubt, the fastest street bike in all of Philly. And because of its custom paint job and custom hand-painted graphics and artwork, it was also the nicest.

Mont pulled the bike up to the garage door and climbed

off it. He strode over to the garage, bent, and unlocked the massive steel sliding doors. He was fortunate to have an older brother with his own garage. It had been he and his brother who did all of the bike's conversions and modifications. But today, there was some tweaking that he had to do before heading to the racetrack to embarrass all of them fools on their Ninjas and Yamahas.

Mont climbed back onto his motorcycle and pulled into the garage. The door closed behind him.

"What the fuck?" Mont turned back toward the door and quickly climbed off his bike. A dark figure emerged from the shadows. "Jerrell!"

Jerrell smiled. "Who'd you think it was? The tooth fairy?"

"What the fuck are you doing here?" Mont asked, surprised. "How in the fuck did you get into the garage?"

"Ancient Chinese secret," Jerrell told him.

Mont's eyes shifted toward the object that Jerrell held in his hand. "Damn, homie! What's up with the pistol?"

"This?" Jerrell held the black Glock up and examined it. "This is for you."

"For me?" Mont asked nervously. "Why for me? Why you drawin', homie?"

"This is a present for you," Jerrell told him. "I want to show you how much I appreciate everything that you did for me while I was locked up."

Mont swallowed hard. "What . . . what are you talking about?"

"Here." Jerrell tossed Mont the gun.

Mont caught the pistol. "Man, what are you doing?"

Jerrell pulled his shirt over his head. "Here, you want my

shirt? You can have the shirt off of my back, Mont." He tossed the shirt to Mont.

Mont caught Jerrell's shirt and held it up. "J, man . . . what are you doing? What are you tripping on?"

"I'm not tripping," Jerrell explained. "I'm just showing you how much love I have for you. I'm just showing how down I am for my niggas."

"We down for you too, J. Junior Mafia forever," Mont replied.

"Oh, yeah?" Jerrell asked. He slowly walked around a metal oil drum with a wrench sitting on top. "Y'all down for me, huh?"

Mont nodded. "Yeah."

"So, where's my fucking money then, Mont?" Jerrell shouted. He lifted the wrench off the drum and threw it at Mont.

"J!" Mont shouted, dodging the wrench. "What the fuck, man?"

"Where's my fucking money, nigga!" Jerrell asked again.

Mont lifted his hands in a calming motion. "J, I got you! Just calm down, I gotcha, baby!"

Jerrell seated himself on the oil drum. "Then where is it?"

"I got it close by," Mont explained. "We can go and get it before I go to the track."

"You sure about that?" Jerrell asked with a smile. He waved his hand around the garage. "Are you sure that you didn't spend it helping your brother get all this?"

Mont swallowed hard and nodded. "Okay. I did go in with my brother on this shop, Jerrell. But I still got some of your money. I didn't use it all. I just needed to borrow some of it to get this place started. But I can give you what I got, and then

I can make payments on the rest. This shop thing is sweet, J! We gonna be making big bucks in here soon."

"So, I gotta wait for my money, 'cause you wanna open up a motorcycle shop?" Jerrell asked. "I gotta wait for my dreams, so that you can take my money and follow yours."

Mont shifted his gaze to the ground.

Jerrell rose from the old rusty oil drum. "What were the rules, Mont? What were the rules about my money?"

Mont lifted his hands again. "J, I . . ."

"I get mines first, and then you can go and spend your shit on whatever you want to!" Jerrell shouted. "You don't go shopping with my shit! You don't buy nothing without paying me first!"

"J, you were locked up!" Mont shouted. "I just figured that I could hit this quick lick, pay you back, and then we would both be cool."

"Why didn't you ask me if you could do that?" Jerrell asked. "Oh, that's right. You couldn't ask me, because you never came to see me. How much money did you say you sent me when I was locked up?"

Mont shook his head.

"And yet, you want to borrow my money without asking and use it to come up?" Jerrell shook his head. "That's a violation of the rules, Mont."

"I'm sorry, J." Mont lifted his shoulders and turned his hands up. "What do you want me to say?"

Jerrell shook his head. "There's nothing left for us to say."

"Just calm down, Jay," Mont said nervously, realizing how shit was going to go down.

Jerrell began walking toward Mont.

"Go on with that bullshit, Jerrell," Mont told him nervously. He lifted the weapon that Jerrell had tossed him. "Stay back, nigga!"

Jerrell laughed and continued his slow walk toward Mont. Mont squeezed the trigger on the Glock and the weapon clicked. He quickly pulled back the slide and released it, and then pulled the trigger again. Nothing happened.

"Nigga, I gave you that gun," Jerrell told him. "Do you think that I'm going to give you a loaded gun to kill me with? Nigga, even I ain't that crazy."

"Man, J, quit tripping!" Mont told him.

"Quit tripping? Nigga, you just tried to do me in!" Jerrell told him. He pulled another weapon from the small of his back and aimed carefully at Mont's right knee.

"No!" Mont shouted.

Jerrell squeezed the trigger and his weapon popped. Mont fell to the ground screaming and holding his knee. Jerrell climbed on top of Mont's motorcycle, turned the ignition, and started the bike up.

"What the fuck are you doing, man?" Mont screamed.

Jerrell carefully maneuvered the bike around the garage until he was just in front of Mont. He raced the engine and propelled the bike forward, riding it on top of his victim.

"Aaaaargh!" Mont screamed like a wounded animal.

Jerrell positioned the rear tire of the motorcycle just on top of Mont's chest, and then revved the engine as high as it could possibly go. Once he had the rims on the ramps and the motor at nine thousand, he released the clutch, allowing the bike to catch first gear. The rear tire spun with the ferocity of a category-five hurricane, shredding skin, tearing flesh, and sending blood and tissue flying through the garage. Mont was dead before the 440-pound bike peeled the meat off his face.

*   *   *

Detective Letoya Ellington stood in the rain, waiting for her charge to show up. He was late, and it pissed her off more than anything else in the world would, for a low-life drug dealer to keep her waiting. As if what they did was so much more important than what she did. Who the fuck were they to keep her waiting? She could see the asshole making his way toward her now.

Rasun approached the detective with a smile on his face. It would be the first time they had met alone. He was glad that she had been put in charge of his case. For one, she was a sister. And two, she was fine as hell. The thought of getting into Detective Ellington's panties had crossed his mind more than once. He wondered how tight police pussy would be, with their uptight asses.

"What the fuck are you smiling at?" Detective Ellington asked.

"You," Rasun told her.

"Maybe you got things twisted," Detective Ellington told him. She kicked Rasun in his nuts, causing him to grab his genitals and buckle. She then slammed him against a nearby brick wall. "Let me make this shit clear to you. You are a low-life fucking drug dealer. And even worse, you're a low-life snitching bitch. You couldn't even stand up and do the time for the crime. So you are lower than low. You're lower than maggot shit, so don't you ever keep me waiting again. You hear me?"

Rasun nodded.

"Good. Now that we got that shit straight, we can get down to business," Detective Ellington told him. "We need to get

Reds on the scene with the drugs. And we need to get him on tape turning the cocaine into crack."

Rasun turned toward the detective. "You want me to wear another wire?"

"We want you to wear another wire," Detective Ellington confirmed. "You got a problem with that? I mean, if it's a problem, we can just let the prosecutors know that you don't want to cooperate with us, and that you just want to go ahead and go to prison for a long fucking time!"

Rasun shook his head. The deal was getting worse and worse, each time that he saw them. They were supposed to be cops, but they rolled like the mob.

"When is Reds going to go to Ms. Shoog's and cook up his stuff?" Detective Ellington asked.

"Tomorrow," Rasun told her. "Damn, did you have to kick me in the nuts?"

"I started to shoot you in them, so be happy," Detective Ellington told him. "So, he's cooking tomorrow. Damn, that means I have to stop raids tonight. Shit!"

"Can I go now?" Rasun asked, still rubbing his sore privates.

"Yeah. Meet us at the deli again in the morning. The same place where we wired you up before. And don't be late. The other detective won't be as nice as I was if you are."

Rasun nodded. "Good to know." He turned and headed out of the alley and down the block. The rain began to pour down even harder. He had betrayed his friends and allowed the man to get his hooks inside him. As part of the deal, he had to give a confession of guilt, on tape, and then sign it in front of a notary. They had him. And if he tried to run, they would catch him and give him thirty years. Or even worse, they would go after his moms again. He was trapped in a cage filled with lying, cheating, low-life hyenas with badges. And they were slowly draining the life out of him, with each of their sinister bites. But what was killing him even more was his betrayal of his friends. Tomorrow he was going to wear a wire. And that wire not only was going to entrap Ms. Shoog, but was going to help the cops solidify their case against his best friend. Tomorrow, he was going to betray someone he considered to be a brother. He was going to betray Reds.

WHATCHA SAYIN'

Rasun walked to the window and peered out. He seemed visibly nervous but no one paid him any mind. He wondered if the police were going to raid the cooking house while they were inside it. *Would Reds shoot, would he run, would Ms. Shoog survive a drug raid? What about a hefty prison sentence? Could Ms. Shoog do time? And what about the cops? How would they come in? Would they run in with guns blazing? Would they toss in a stun grenade, blowing out everyone's eardrums?*

"Goddamn. Shoog, what the fuck is that smell?" Reds asked.

Ms. Shoog shook her head sadly. "Child, my washing machine is gone out, baby."

"Damn!" Pookey said, waving his hands around. "That shit smells foul!"

"Can we get a window open in here?" Dontae asked.

"Yeah, why not open up all a the doors too!" Amar said sarcastically. "We ain't doing nothing but cooking up some coke!"

Ms. Shoog shuffled across the floor to her laundry room and opened the door, allowing the smell of spoiled clothing to waft into the room. Amar, Reds, Rasun, Dontae, and Pookey all raced for the closest windows.

"Sorry, but y'all better get used to the smell," Ms. Shoog told them. "Maybe if y'all pay me this time, I can go ahead and get a new one."

Reds took his shirt off and tied it around his mouth. "Goddamn, Shoog! Okay, a nigga a handle that shit!"

"For real!" Amar told her. He reached into his pocket, peeled off a couple of hundred-dollar bills, and handed them to her.

"Here!" Rasun handed her two hundred-dollar bills as well.

Reds reached into his pocket and pulled out a thick wad of money. He pulled off three one-hundred-dollar bills and handed them to her.

"Here, get that shit taken care of with the quickness."

Shoog turned toward Pookey and stared at him sadly. "Washing machines is just so damn expensive these days."

Pookey shook his head and pulled out a fat wad. He pulled off three bills and handed them to Ms. Shoog. Just when you thought she was cool, that's when she really hit they asses up.

"But it's that dryer that's broke down," Ms. Shoog told them. "I can't dry no clothes, and that's how they get so spoiled."

Dontae shook his head and smiled. "Here, old woman! You sure got a lot a game."

Ms. Shoog took Dontae's three hundred dollars and added it to her collection. She closed the laundry room and tucked her money away in her bra. "Thank you, babies! Now Ms. Shoog can have it all nice and sweet smelling in here for y'all."

Reds and Rasun exchanged knowing smiles.

"Okay, okay, can we just get down to business?" Reds asked.

Ms. Shoog shuffled over to her stove and turned on two of the burners. "You know Ms. Shoog is still the best at this shit, don'tcha?"

Amar turned away from the window. "Yo, here come that nigga Rik!"

Pookey unlatched the door and opened it. Rik walked through it and tossed his gym bag onto the coffee table.

"Shoog, what's the line look like?" Rik shouted into the kitchen.

"I'm hooking up Reds and Ra, and then Pookey, and then Amar, and then Dontae, and then you're next, baby," Shoog told him.

Rik seated himself on the couch, leaned forward, and un-zipped his gym bag. He pulled out kilo after kilo from the extra-large bag and set them down on the table.

"Damn, you niggas need to get ya own damn cook!" Rik told them with a smile. "Y'all monopolizing my shit. Ain't that right, Shoog?"

"That's right, baby!" Shoog shouted from the kitchen.

"Then you should have paid for her damn new washing machine and dryer," Reds told him.

Rik laughed. "Word? She hit you niggas up like that?"

"Hell yeah," Amar said, smacking his lips.

Rik shook his head and laughed. "Damn, that old woman got game! What story she sell y'all this time?"

"Her fucking washing machine and dryer broke down," Amar told him.

"And that's why it's funky as a muthafucka in here," Dontae added.

Rik laughed and clapped his hands together. "Damn! The washer and dryer broke at the same time? Shoog, you'se a bad muthafucka yo!"

"Hell, I bought 'em at the same time, so they broke down at the same time!" Shoog shouted back from the kitchen.

Rasun strolled into the kitchen where Ms. Shoog was preparing her materials.

"Rasun, hand me that big Pyrex dish on the table, baby," Ms. Shoog told him.

Rasun handed Shoog the dish. She busted open one of the kilos of cocaine and poured it into the dish, then set the dish on the stove.

"Ms. Shoog don't use none of that microwave shit, baby," she told him. "I don't need you to tell me what to do, fool, I got this. I do this shit the old-fashion way!"

Ms. Shoog added a cup of lukewarm water to the cocaine, then lifted a large spatula that she had next to the stove and began to stir the mixture. The fire from the stove began to melt the drugs, turning the substance into a thick, oily, yellowish gook. Ms. Shoog stirred the oily concoction, adding a second cup of water, and then an unusually large amount of baking soda. The yellowish gook quickly turned into a thick white substance with the consistency of finely blended cake mix.

Ms. Shoog turned toward Rasun and smiled. "This is how you want it, baby."

Rasun examined the pasty substance and nodded.

Ms. Shoog pointed to a stack of glass dishes on the side of the counter. "Hand me another one of those dishes, baby."

Rasun handed Ms. Shoog another glass Pyrex dish. Ms. Shoog took the dish, busted open a kilo, and poured it into the container. She set the dish on the stove and poured in a large cup of water.

"How long you been cooking coke, Ms. Shoog? 'Cause you sure do know what you're doing." Rasun asked, stroking her so she would answer.

"Baby, Ms. Shoog been cooking for a long time," she told him, slowly turning her mixture. She poured in a second cup of water and added a large amount of baking soda. "Probably before you was born."

Rasun felt the wire taped to his chest. He knew what he had to do, and he hated every second of it. But it was either Shoog or his mother. "So, Shoog, how much shit you gotta cook up for these niggas today?"

"Hell, Reds, Rik, Amar brought six, Dante brought four with his broke ass." Ms. Shoog pulled the dish off the fire and set it to the side, next to the first dish. She then reached for a third. "Pookey with his po' self want me to cook up four."

"Shit, that ain't nothing compared to the damage Quadir use to do. Shoot, if he was here, you'd be here all day cooking," Rasun said with a smile.

Ms. Shoog laughed. "Oh, that boy would have me busy for two days cooking all of his shit! I'll never forget that time Quadir brought me two hundred keys and wanted it all cooked in two days! Hell, I felt like Sara Lee up in this bitch!"

Rasun laughed. He had enough information from Ms. Shoog. It was now time to concentrate on Rik. He turned and headed into the living room to find his next victim.

"So, the bitch stuck her head under the covers trying to fade a nigga, but I couldn't hold that shit any longer!" Dontae said, laughing. "She came up mad as a muthafucka, choking and gasping for air and shit!"

The guys gathered around the living room bust into laughter.

"Man, how could you mess that up?" Pookey asked. "That bitch is finer than a muthafucka! Nigga, I been trying to knock that since day one, and you fuck it off by gassing the bitch!"

Rik threw his head back in laughter.

Rasun walked to the table where Rik had his kilos stacked up. He lifted one of the bricks. "Damn, nigga. How much dope is this?"

"Twenty birds, nigga," Rik told him. "I got thirty more in the ride. I need to have this shit ready for the first of the month."

"It's the first of the month," Pookey said, singing. "It's the first of the month."

"What the fuck you cooking up all that shit at once for?" Rasun asked.

"Because, nigga, I got customers," Rik explained. "I'm expanding into some very lucrative territory. Them Junior Mafia niggas have been dropping like flies in the wintertime, and all of their peeps have been calling me trying to get something. Nigga, this shit won't last me four days the way my phone ringing off the hook!"

"You willing to risk a war with them crazy Junior Mafia dudes? That Jerrell Jackson is a fucking nut case. I heard that nigga knocking everybody right now over his money that got fucked up while he was locked up," Reds said.

"Ain't gonna be no war," Rik told him. "Them niggas is so paranoid right now, they are all running scared for hiding like some little bitches. Them niggas don't know who's reaching out and touching they ass, so they ain't trying to do nothing to nobody right now."

Rasun nodded. He was finished with his questions for now. He was sure that he had given his slave master more than enough. Now, he just wanted this shit to be over. He wanted this to be the last time he had to do this shit, because it was making him sick to his stomach. And the wire-wearing shit had to cease. That shit made him nervous. What if a nigga hugged him too tight or something? He just stayed nervous the whole time he had the damn thing on. This morning, he had to pull over the side of the road and jump out of the car. His stomach wouldn't hold his breakfast down, that's how nervous he was. Not to mention, ever since he had gotten locked up and started fucking with the clown-ass task force, his hair was falling out, he was constantly throwing up, some days he'd have diarrhea, and if that wasn't bad enough he was literally starting to feel like he was coming down with the flu, just plain ol' physically sick. Snitching was like a corrosive poison that was eating him up from the inside, like a deadly malignant cancer. If it ended up killing him, he wouldn't complain about that either.

Crawling under a rock and dying was something that he truly felt like doing. He had betrayed his friends, his boys, his crew. These were the niggas that he had grown up with. The niggas that he had come up in the game with, his boys who had had his back since kindergarten, and now he was about to fuck them all over.

Rasun could feel himself growing nauseated once again.

Sweat started pouring down his face, his mouth became moist, and his head began swirling. He raced for Ms. Shoog's bathroom.

"What the fuck's wrong with that nigga?" Pookey asked.

"Probably that fucked-up smell still getting to him," Amar told him.

In the van down the street, Detective Ellington stacked her papers together and removed her headphones. She had heard enough. Rasun had given them more than enough. This case was a wrap. Everyone in that room would be arrested and indicted within twenty-four hours.

DON'T STOP GET IT GET IT

Gena lifted her head from her steering wheel. She was parked in the neighborhood Pathmark parking lot just sitting, quiet and still. She watched people pass by—cars, kids, shopping carts—and she simply tried to digest what she had heard her cousin say. *That's why your father killed your mother.* Gena couldn't imagine the thought. It was just something to think about. *That's why Daddy's in jail. Why the fuck they say he tried to rob a bank for? Why didn't they just tell me the truth?* Yes, the truth would have been better, it always is. Truth is a hard thing, but maybe harder is sometimes better than betrayal. And right now Gena felt so betrayed by her family that she questioned her entire existence. *I bet everybody knows too.* Gena picked up her phone and tried to call her cousin Gary, but again she got another voice mail.

"Dag, don't nobody answer their phones when you need them."

She didn't want to call the house. *What if Aunt Paula answers the phone?* She tried Gary's cell phone once more, refusing the confrontation with Gary's mother, but still no answer. She needed someone to talk to, someone to tell that her whole life was a lie, her mother's death and her father's imprisonment were one and the same and that her entire family knew and she had not one clue. *There's something extremely wrong with this and with my family for doing that to me.* She felt so betrayed. *I wish you was here, Quadir, I really do.*

Just then her phone rang. She looked at the number. It was Jay. She had forgotten they had an early dinner date. She answered the phone and confirmed she was on her way. His call had come with perfect timing. Gena needed company and the truth was Quadir wasn't there. *Jay don't seem that bad. He could be Mr. Replacement.* She revved up her engine and exited the parking lot to meet Jay for dinner. He had turned out to be everything that she had ever wanted in a man. He was kind, and sensitive, and handsome, and polite. He listened to her when she talked. He opened doors for her when they went out. He would call her to say goodnight, or to tell her how beautiful she was.

She didn't care about his money, but he did appear to have some change. That nice baby blue Range Rover that he was pushing definitely wasn't cheap. Plus he was jeweled out. His apartment was in a real swanky part of town and even had a doorman. Jay had an expensively decorated home with fine furnishing and lavish silk tapestries. He had it all. And when they went out, he never ever let her pay for anything. He always paid for dinner, and the little gifts that he gave her were always nice. But she knew he wasn't holding like Quadir. His paper was way short compared to Quadir. Actually, it wasn't fair to Jay to even try to compare ballin' status. But it didn't matter; she had plenty of money. She liked him just because he was nice and attentive. Jay was smart too. He had a nice vocabulary, and he used words that the average fella on the street didn't. And he was also a bit mysterious, and even dangerous. She couldn't resist.

The look that they got when they were out on the street told her that she had a real man. The other guys on the street deferred to him when they walked along the sidewalk or into a restaurant. He was a natural leader. He kept himself well groomed and smelling nice. And he could kiss like there was no tomorrow. She would become lost inside his strong lips. When they kissed, it often felt as if she were standing on a cliff peering over it, with only him to keep her from falling.

She reached the corner and held her breath. It was here where the black BMW always waited for her. Each time that she turned this corner, she held her breath as fear gripped her. Fortunately, today wasn't one of those days. The black Beemer was nowhere to be found.

Gena rounded the corner and headed out of the neighborhood. She was so happy that she hadn't seen the black Beemer waiting to follow her today that she completely missed the magenta Jaguar that pulled in behind her. She turned up the stereo and blissfully became lost in her Mary J. Blige CD, unaware that she had picked up a tail.

Champagne exited her red Alfa Romeo Spider and strutted to where her meeting was to take place. She could see him standing near the park bench waiting impatiently. He looked good to her still, but she wasn't going to let all his looks, his smile, or his charm overtake her. She had fallen for those things before, too many times, in the past. And each time, she had found herself being hurt. Perhaps that was why she now had a heart as hard as steel.

"What took you so long?" Jerrell demanded. He eyed Champagne closely. She still looked like she could be on the cover of a beauty magazine, or on a stage twirling down a pole in Atlanta. She had a natural beauty about her, but it was a beauty that could switch from wholesome to seductive with the addition of a little makeup and a change in hairstyle. Champagne had been the girl of his dreams at one time. She was actually one of the few women he ever trusted. Their relationship lasted less than six months, but their friendship had developed over time. He had known Champagne now for about fifteen years and she was a trouper, a true soldier, and one of the few people he could still turn to. Had life been fair, she would still be his woman. But life was far from fair. And unfortunately, she had too much water under the bridge to ever be anyone's wife.

"I got here when I got here," Champagne said gruffly. "What do you want now? What is it this time? More guns to hide? An alibi for some detective? What?"

Jerrell smiled and shook his head. "Damn, why does it always have to be like that?"

"Because with you, it has to be," Champagne told him. "With you there's always some bullshit involved. With you there's always a motive."

"Was I really that bad?" Jerrell asked. "I mean, you acting like a brother be straight wilding out. You acting like I only call you when I need something foul."

Champagne put her hands on her hips.

Jerrell smiled again. "Glad to know all of the love is still there."

"What the fuck do you want, Jerrell?" she asked.

Jerrell exhaled, reached into his pocket, and pulled out the photo of Gena that he had taken at the restaurant. "You know her?"

"What the fuck do I look like, information or something?"

"You know everybody," Jerrell told her. "I just figured you might have screwed the same baller once or twice. You know how you ho's move in small circles."

"Fuck you, you black bitch," Champagne told him. "I know one asshole that I wish I had never screwed."

"Don't get your dirty little panties all in a bunch, ma," Jerrell told her. "Do you know the bitch or not?"

Champagne crossed her arms and squinted at Jerrell. "And if I did know her, what of it?"

"I just want some information, that's all."

Champagne snatched the picture away from Jerrell and examined it.

"Well?" Jerrell asked impatiently.

Champagne shook her head. "She looks familiar. Yeah, I've seen her around."

"Around?" Jerrell grew more animated. "Where?"

Champagne shrugged. "Just around. Clubs, parties, the mall, who the fuck knows? I've seen the bitch. What's it to you?"

"I need for you to concentrate," Jerrell told her. "I need for you to focus. Where have you seen her, and with who?"

"What is she, a new piece of pussy?" Champagne asked. "Some bitch who's got you all twisted up, and now you think she's stepping out on you?"

Jerrell shook his head. "That shit doesn't matter. I just need you to do what you do. Find out everything that you can about this bitch and get back to me. I want to know every fucking thing that you can dig up. If she lost a fucking tooth in third grade, I want to know about it. I want to know where she lives, where she went to school, and who she fucks with or has fucked with."

Champagne smirked and tucked the picture into her bra. "You know this is going to cost you."

"The usual?"

Champagne shook her head. "Uh-un. Something tells me that this one is a lot more valuable to you. I want a thousand for this one."

"A thousand dollars!" Jerrell shouted. "Bitch, you must be crazy! A thousand dollars? Have you lost your muthafuckin' mind?"

"Take it or leave it, bitch," Champagne told him. "I would have charged you less, but you don't know how to shut the fuck up. That dirty panty comment is gonna cost, nigga."

Jerrell frowned and pursed his lips. "Okay. You got that. You get me what I want, and I'll give you what you want."

"Don't call me, I'll call you," Champagne told him. She turned and strutted across the street to her waiting Alfa Romeo.

Gena pulled up to the park and spied the voluptuous woman strutting away from her man. She frowned as she thought of the possibilities. *Who the fuck is she? What the fuck is he out here doing?* She rushed toward Jerrell with a fierce scowl on her face.

"Who was that?" Gena asked.

"Nobody."

"Nobody?" Gena turned toward Champagne, who was

driving past them. "She didn't seem like a nobody. You were all up in her ass while she was walking away!"

"Gena, that was my cousin!" Jerrell shouted.

"Bullshit!"

"She was!" Jerrell shouted. "She saw me standing here waiting on you, and she pulled over, got out of the car, and came over and said what's up to me."

Gena crossed her arms and shook her head. "Jay, you are so full of shit. I don't even know why I allowed myself to fall for you. I should have known that you were just like all of the rest!"

"Gena, I swear to you!" Jerrell said forcefully. "Why would I meet another woman here, knowing that you were on your way? Think about that shit, will you? Why would I do that?" he asked, even though that was exactly what he had done.

Gena shifted her weight to one side and exhaled.

"Gena, if I was going to creep on you, do you honestly think that I would do it here, in the middle of a park that you are coming to, in broad daylight? Think about that!"

Gena lowered her head and nodded. He was making sense. And she hadn't actually caught him doing anything out of line.

"You know what, Jay?" Gena told him. "That bitch better be at your next family reunion or Christmas party or Thanksgiving dinner or I'm fucking you and your mans up! You hear me?" she said, grabbing his dick.

Jerrell smiled and nodded. "I hear you, baby. Damn, you threatening a nigga's Johnson and shit, acting like you own the muthafucka."

"I do own that muthafucka." Gena smiled. "That bitch belongs to me, and don't you forget it."

"Damn, baby," Jerrell said, pulling her close. "I've been waiting for you to claim ownership. You know that you can take possession of this muthafucka wherever you want to."

Gena nodded. "I just might do that. I just might do that."

Jerrell plunged into Gena with the force of a high diver hitting the pool. And like the diver he plunged inside her, swimming inside her, causing her to gasp for air. Gena opened her legs wider, trying to ease the pain. It just made him go deeper into her, causing her to cry out.

Jerrell had waited for this day since meeting her at the gas station, and for the past weeks, he had waited patiently, cunningly plotting how he would get her to fall for him. He played a role like the Hollywood hustler he was, all because he wanted to tap this fat caramel-colored ass so bad that he could taste it. He let her know how bad he wanted her, with every punishing stroke that he delivered. He made her regret that she had made him wait so long. Week after week, shit, damn near two months since they first met. Gena placed her hands beneath his stomach as he stroked, in an effort to diffuse some of the pain. He was hitting it, and hitting it hard. *Wow, it's been so long, he's so big, shit's incredible.* She grabbed the sheets first, and then the pillow, and finally his waist. She dug her fingernails into his sides, trying to take the pain that he was dishing out. She hadn't been with a man since Quadir, and now she was paying dearly for it.

Jerrell kept pounding relentlessly with what seemed to be a much bigger penis than she was used to, trying to go deeper and deeper with each stroke. He could feel every inch of her depth with each of his movements. She was tight as a balled-up fist, and she pulled and tugged at his manhood with each of his strokes. He could feel her tight walls wrapped around him, and he didn't know how much longer he would be able to take it. *Damn, she got some good pussy,* Jerrell couldn't help thinking to himself.

Gena wrapped her legs around Jerrell and pulled him down on top of her. No sooner had she done it than she realized her mistake. At least when he was pounding her, he was pulling it out a little. Now that pounding had turned into a deep gut-churning grind. She exploded and cried out in his ear. She could feel him all the way inside her stomach.

Gena's fingernails dug deep into Jerrell's back, while her teeth found their way to his sweating neck. He had been grinding relentlessly for the last ten minutes, and her insides felt as if they were on fire. The pounding that he had given her the first fifteen minutes had made her cervix soar, but the deep-ass punishment that he was putting on her now felt as if it were twisting her guts into a knot. Besides, she had come six times, and she was beginning to get a headache.

Gena could feel goose bumps beginning to appear on Jerrell's back, and if they meant the same thing on him that they had meant on Quadir, then that meant that he was about to get his. And sure enough he did. Jerrell exploded inside Gena like a volcano erupting. His warm white lava flew deep up inside her, causing her to cry out and come again herself. She could feel his massive member vibrating inside her as it released its load. Jerrell remained stiff on top of her for one more minute, until the throbbing from his penis stopped, and then his entire body went limp. He relaxed on top of her, and she felt some relief inside her vagina as his manhood retreated to a decent size.

Gena caressed Jerrell's shoulder and smiled. She wondered if she would be able to take this kind of punishment every night, if they moved in together. The tingling sensation in her body gave her the answer. *Hell yeah!*

Jerrell rolled over and lay on the bed beside her. She was glad, because she was tired. He had given her ass more than a workout. He had done something that a man hadn't done in a long while. He had fucked her to sleep. She rolled over, wrapping the blankets around her body, and fell fast asleep.

SHE'LL BE COMIN' ROUND THE MOUNTAIN

United States District Attorney Paul Perachetti paced in front of the room filled to the brim with various law enforcement agents, officers, and deputies.

Captain Holiday of the Philadelphia Police Department cleared his throat. "I want to thank all of our fellow agencies, departments, and bureaus for coming out today and helping us out. Gentleman, zero hour is almost on us. I'll keep my remarks brief for now. At this time, for those of you who don't know him, I would like to bring up United States District Attorney of the Western District of Pennsylvania, Mr. Paul Perachetti."

"Gentleman, and ladies, I want to thank you all for being here today, and I want to thank you all for the enormous amount of effort and sacrifice that you've put forward over the preceding months," Perachetti told the gathered crowd. "Some of you have worked this case for more than a year.

You've sacrificed much to uphold the laws of our country, and to make the streets safe once again. I know that over the past year there have been many missed dinners, missed birthdays, missed plays and school recitals, and a lot of strained families. Your deeds will not go unrewarded.

"Today, we have a really big day ahead of us," Mr. Perachetti continued. "Today we will be executing some fifty search warrants simultaneously. This will be the biggest drug sting in the history of the State of Pennsylvania. I just wanted to thank all of the participating agencies. Captain Holiday and the Philadelphia Police Department deserve a round of applause for doing the warrants, managing the confidential informants, and these guys really really are who made today possible."

The officers and agents gathered around the room broke into applause.

"I would like to thank Special Agent in Charge Rudy Galvani, of the FBI," Perachetti continued. "I want to thank Agent Stacey Wynn, of the Drug Enforcement Administration, and I want to thank Colonel Whitfield of the Pennsylvania National Guard."

The law enforcement officers gathered around the room applauded their fellow officers.

"Colonel Whitfield contacted the governor's office and assisted us in obtaining permission to use his National Guard troops to help conduct the search and seizure, and we also have their full assistance in rounding up the perpetrators," Perachetti informed them. "Without the Guard, we would not have enough manpower to raid all fifty of the facilities simultaneously. So they certainly have our deepest appreciation."

Again the officers and agents applauded.

"I just want to thank the Sheriff's Department, and the Pennsylvania State Troopers Office, as well as the United States Border Patrol, and the United States Customs Agency, for loaning us their narcotics canines," Perachetti continued. "I'll turn it back over to Captain Holiday so that he can wrap things up. I just wanted to thank everyone who made today possible. Be careful out there, gentlemen and ladies."

Perachetti left the podium and Captain Holiday stepped behind the microphone. The officers inside the room gave another loud round of applause of gratitude and then grew silent again.

"Gentlemen, what we are doing today will have a direct correlation to the amount of drugs that make it on to the streets of Philadelphia this year," Captain Holiday told them. "This operation will net real results, and will undoubtedly result in numerous convictions of some of Philadelphia's most notorious drug dealers. Those of you who know me know that I am not prone to real emotional speeches. So I'll just keep it short and sweet. Go out there and kick some ass, guys. Be careful, watch each other's back, and everyone go home to your families tonight. I'll give up the stage now to the detectives who put this thing together, and who are coordinating today's operation, Detectives Ellington and Ratzinger."

Detective Ratzinger stood just behind the podium, allowing Detective Ellington to have the microphone. Whistles shot through the room.

"All right, all right, wise guys," Detective Ellington waved them off. "Keep it down before I tell your wives."

Laughter shot through the room.

"Listen up, guys, we're doing fifty houses all at the same time. That means fifty teams. We're dividing the operations

into sections. There will be five section leaders, each with
ten teams. Each team will consist of ten to fifteen officers,
agents, deputies, or Guardsmen. We have already organized
the teams, and we'll be passing out team lists, so everyone
will know what team they'll belong to. We'll have time to do
some runthroughs over at the Academy, and at the National
Guard Training Center. We'll cycle the teams through, so
that everyone will have the opportunity to run an operation
and get to know their team members. These are search warrants and arrest warrants. I want everyone to make sure that
these suspects get their Miranda rights read to them as soon
as the premises are secure. I don't want anything thrown out
because of a Miranda violation. Gentlemen and ladies, this
operation is a go. Get your teams together and to the training
sites so that we can prep for the operation. That's about it.
Good luck."

"We are operating on channel five, gentlemen," Detective
Ratzinger shouted. "Make sure that your radios are on secure
link five!"

The officers and agents broke up and headed off to their
gathering points.

"Hey, what do you think you're doing?" asked Gena playfully
as she watched Jay sit next to her with a bottle of massaging
oil in his hands.

"Smelling your feet?" he said as he picked up her big toe
with his thumb and pointer finger and held her foot up in
the air as if it were a dirty diaper. "I can't be handling fungus,
you feel me?"

"Fungus . . . boy, you see these toes?" she asked, holding

her feet up to his face. "Look at 'em. Tell the truth, aren't these the most perfect feet you ever seen in your life?"

Truthfully, they really were tiny, small, perfect feet and toes and they turned him on. Actually, everything about Gena turned him on. She had a lot going on with her family and when she asked if she could stay with him, just for a while until she found her own place, he thought he would mind. He said yes, but at the time he didn't really mean it, and further, he really didn't want her that close to him. But because of the family situation, he said okay, thinking that she'd just be there for a few days. But a few days had turned into a few weeks. And he liked it. He didn't think he would, but he did, and he wasn't looking forward to her leaving.

Gena would wake up in the mornings and be out the door before 8:30 A.M. to run her own errands and take care of her own business. He didn't give her a key, but he accommodated her comings and goings. There were times when he'd even come home just to unlock the door for her, and then go back out to whatever it was he was doing. He gave her little amounts of shopping money, even though he had already figured out she was holding the bread and the butter. They'd wake, shower, eat, and roll out, and at night, they'd watch movies or play spades, which had become Jerrell's favorite pastime while he was incarcerated waiting for his trial.

"Want to play cards?" he asked after rubbing her feet.

"Again?"

"Yeah, come on."

She had never played cards as much as she did since she met him. And the thing was it was bad enough that she didn't want to play, but then he'd make her gamble and take her money if she lost.

"You know you giving that back, right?" asked Gena as she watched Jerrell throw the cards down and swipe away a hundred dollars off the table.

"Shit, my ass. You snooze you lose, babe."

"Whatever, Jay, whatever," she said, watching as he counted his winnings.

For the most part, it was a little vacation from the reality of Richard Allen, but Gena knew she would not stay long. No, after Jamal threw her out, then Viola threw her out, Gena had decided that shit wouldn't be happening ever again. As comfortable as she was in Jay's house, she knew she could not stay and didn't want to wear out her welcome either. So, for the past couple of weeks, she had been apartment hunting and looking at several condos in the Old City section of Philadelphia near South Street.

Jerrell had gotten quite used to her womanly touch. Truthfully, while he didn't want her there in the beginning, he now couldn't imagine her not around. Plus, he liked being able to keep track of his newfound investment. He knew that in the end, putting his time in with her would be worth his while, he just didn't know how worth his while she'd turn out to be.

Rasun woke up sweating in the darkness. He could feel it rising from his stomach to his throat. He swallowed hard to keep it down, but found that it did not work. And once again he found himself racing to the bathroom and kneeling in front of the toilet.

"Strap my chinstrap for me," SWAT team leader Johnny Wang asked Detective Ellington.

Letoya Ellington shook her head. "Johnny, I'll bet your mommy still dresses you in the morning, doesn't she?"

"She wouldn't have to if you would let me move in with your fine ass," Lieutenant Wang said with a smile.

"Johnny, you couldn't handle this pussy if I tied both hands behind my back," Detective Ellington told him.

The SWAT team members gathered around them broke into laughter. Detective Ellington checked the magazine in her weapon, and then cocked it, chambering a round. She checked her black Kevlar vest, her tactical utility belt, and her communications radio. Like all of the other officers and agents participating in the predawn raids, she was dressed in all-black paramilitary gear, with a black mask over her face, black gloves on her hands, black knee and elbow pads, and a variety of other gear.

Detective Ellington lifted her black Kevlar helmet and strapped it onto her head. "Okay, listen up everyone, comm-link check! Team leader, check your communications. Remember, we are operating on secure link five!"

Detective Ellington lifted the microphone attached to the shoulder strap on her bulletproof vest. "Section leaders, this is Command One. Have your team leaders acknowledge."

Letoya turned to Lieutenant Ratzinger. "Hey, Mark. When they report in, make sure that they all did their comm check. And synchronize on me. We are go in T minus four minutes."

Detective Ratzinger nodded. "Roger that, sweet lady. You just make sure that you keep your head down in there. You let SWAT go in first."

Detective Ellington caressed Mark's cheek. "Aw, you worry

about me too much, old man. I've done this too many times to play the hero."

"My team's all loaded up and ready to rock 'n' roll," Team Leader Wang told her.

Detective Ellington nodded. "Well, let's load up and get rolling."

Letoya Ellington adjusted her helmet and climbed into the back of the SWAT truck, just behind Lieutenant Wang. She checked her watch.

"Two minutes to showtime," Johnny Wang told her.

Detective Ellington clicked the button on her walkie-talkie. "Section leaders, this is Command. We are two minutes to show time. All sections, we are a go. You have tactical command at this time. I repeat, all section leaders have tactical command at this time. You may begin operations at this time."

Johnny Wang turned toward his driver. "Move out. Get us to the door, Bobby!"

The SWAT van pulled out of the parking lot and rounded the corner. It was 3:00 A.M., and the entire neighborhood seemed deserted. The target's house was just down the street, and they would be there in less than twenty seconds.

"Target looks quiet, sir," a voice declared over Lieutenant Wang's communications link. "Looks like we have achieved tactical surprise," he said, loving every minute of his job.

Lieutenant Wang nodded and keyed his walkie-talkie twice, acknowledging the last transmission. He rose from his seat and threw open the doors to the SWAT van. His men poured out of the van and raced to the front door. One of the team members raced to the left side of the house, while another raced to the right side. They wanted to make sure that no one escaped out of the sides of the house. Three of the team members raced to the backyard to secure the rear of the premises. The others gathered on the sides of the front door, while the team member holding the steel battering ram raced to the front door and smashed it open. SWAT team members poured into the house like ants.

Rik bolted from sleep when he heard the door being smashed open. He jumped out of bed just as the first SWAT team member was entering his bedroom. The masked, black-clad agent was standing behind a large black bulletproof shield that had SWAT painted on it in big white letters. Rik could see the officer's black Sig Sauer semiautomatic handgun sticking out of the gun slit in the center of the shield.

"Police department!" the officer shouted. "We have a search warrant! Get down on the floor now!"

Rik lifted his hands into the air.

"Get down on the floor now!" the officer shouted again.

Slowly, Rik dropped to his knees and lay facedown on the floor. He could feel himself being handcuffed.

Agent Ellington strolled into the room, just as two SWAT team members were lifting a handcuffed Rik off the floor.

"Good morning, Tyrik!" Detective Ellington said with a smile. "You look sleepy. Did we disturb you?"

Ms. Shoog was sound asleep when she heard the explosion and then smoke poured into her bedroom.

"What the fuck is going on?" Shoog shouted. She searched her nightstand for her glasses. Once she finally located them, put them on, and turned toward her bedroom door, she found that she was no longer alone. Her room was now filled with men wearing camouflage uniforms, all pointing M-16 rifles at her.

"I was gonna pay my taxes, I was just a little late with the money, that's all," Shoog told them.

Detective Dick Davis strolled into Shoog's bedroom holding a pair of handcuffs up in the air. "This isn't about your taxes, ma'am. This is about you being the Betty Crocker of the hood for all of the local dope dealers."

"Oh, no, son, you got the wrong lady!" Shoog shook her head. "Mmm mmm, that ain't me, no, sir." And if you didn't know better, you would have believed her.

"Are you kidding me? We know you're the right person, Alvetta Clark. Now get her downstairs into the truck," he said, motioning to another officer.

"All right now, if I got to be going somewhere, do you think I could get dressed? Come on, now, y'all step outta here and let an old woman get dressed," she said, smiling and pretending, her usual.

Detective Davis smiled. "We figured you might say something like that, Ms. Clark or Ms. Shoog, whoever you are. I want you to meet my friend Irma. She's from the Pennsylvania National Guard, and she's going to do a body search for us."

A massive, stocky, six-foot-two-inch woman wearing camouflage makeup on her face stomped through the crowd of soldiers and smiled at Shoog. Irma was missing two teeth in the front.

Ohmigod, look at this mountain bitch I got to deal with. Damn, damn, damn, Ms. Shoog thought, but she heard Michael Shawn as the mountain bitch frisked her ass, handcuffed her, and hauled her ass away into the back of a paddy wagon.

DO I DO

LeChevue was the place everybody seemed to pile into. Everybody knew everybody at LeChevue and the ballers' wives would socialize and get their hair and nails done. It was the place where the wives and girlfriends of the NFL's Eagles or NBA's 76ers went to flaunt their hundred-thousand-dollar cars and multikarat rings. It was the shop of the young, black, and elite. It was where Gena had been going for years.

Gena and Markita, her old neighbor from Chancellor Street, walked into the shop, and to her surprise, she found many of her old friends inside. They immediately went into shouting, howling, and wailing mode.

"Gena!" Bridgette shouted. "Girrrrrl, where have you been?"

Gena raced to the seat where Pam was waiting, leaned forward, and hugged her.

"Girl, I can't believe it!" Beverly wailed. "Ms. Gena is back in the house! Girl, what you been doing to your hair? Gena, you let somebody else do your hair or something 'cause this ain't my work."

"No, nut, I been doing it myself," she said, hugging Beverly. "How's you and Quinny Day?"

"Aw, we good, we good. What about you, though? Man, it's been months. You just stopped coming around."

"I know, I know, I needed some time, that's all. I'm good though."

"Well, your hair ain't. You did this?"

Gena laughed and shook her head. "Girl, you know I don't let nobody up in this mess but you. I've been trying to keep it up."

Gena definitely wasn't going to tell them that she had been trying to lie low for a while, once she found Qua's money. These gossiping whores would have her business all over the East Coast.

"Hey, baby!" Veronica rose, waddled to where Gena was, and hugged her.

Gena placed her hand on Veronica's stomach. "Girl, let me find out?"

"I know, that nigga Rik got me all fucked up, girl. I can't wait till this baby pop out so I can get back to my life. Shit, I can't go to no clubs like this."

"Club? Honey, you don't even look like you can make it out the front door and you worried about the club?" joked Gena.

The girls around the shop broke into laughter.

"Hey, y'all, this is my friend, Markita. She used to be my neighbor out west." Gena introduced, while clasping Markita's arm. "Kita, this is Veronica, and that's Bridgette, and that's Beverly, that's big-head Val over there, and that's Tracey."

Markita waved at everyone and seated herself in the waiting area. Gena made her way around the shop exchanging hugs with everybody.

"Gena, what the hell is that you are driving?" Tracey asked, peering out of the shop's glass front windows.

"Girl, that's the Catch Me if You Can Porsche out there." Gena smiled, patting her hair coquettishly.

"Uh-un, girl!" Beverly waited. "No you didn't go and knock off one of them!"

"Girl, that car is too fly!" Veronica shouted as she and Tina high-fived one another.

"Girl, what's his name?" Tina asked. "And does he have a brother?"

Gena threw her head back in laughter. "Girl, please!"

"What's his name, Gena?" Beverly asked.

"What?" Gena smiled uncontrollably.

Beverly squinted at Gena for several moments. "Ummmmm-hmmm. Girl, I've known you for too long. What's his name? All of a sudden you outside and you ballin'? Bitch, I know better. Either Quadir is back from the dead or you done stumbled upon a winning lottery ticket."

Gena laughed and turned her palms up toward the ceiling. "What are you talking about?"

Tina rose and walked over to Gena and began to sniff her. "Uh-un, girl. I smell dick on you, too."

Laughter shot around the beauty shop.

Gena shoved Tina away, "Bitch, get yo ass away from me."

"What's his name, Gena!" Pam shouted. "Don't change the subject."

"Girl, your face is clear, you can't stop smiling, you got a new car, and you ain't been coming around," Val told her. "Girl, you getting some dick. And it must be some good dick!"

Again, the ladies around the beauty shop broke into laughter.

Gena nodded. "Okay, I see what this is. This is clown Gena day, huh?"

"All you have to do is tell us 'bout Mr. Put a Smile on Your Face," Beverly told her.

Gena shook her head. "Jay. His name is Jay, okay?"

"Oooooh, Jay!" Tina said, pronouncing his name dramatically.

"Where's this nigga from?" Beverly asked bluntly.

The ladies around the shop broke into laughter again.

"He's from Philly," Gena told them bashfully.

"Is he a baller?" Pam asked.

"Something like that," Gena told them. "He don't need no money, I can tell you that."

"Well, all I want to know is he good in the bed?" Veronica asked. "Shoot, can the nigga fuck? 'Cause God knows they not worth nothing else."

Gena turned toward Veronica. "Bitch, that's why you like that now. Close ya legs, and stop thinking about dick."

"What else is there to think about?" Veronica asked looking at her like she was crazy. She high-fived Tina. "Dick and money, money and dick. Those are the only things niggas are good for."

Val called for Markita to sit at her station. It was her first time at the shop, so she didn't have a regular beautician yet. Beverly waved for Gena to come over and sit down in her chair.

"So, what do you want to do to this stuff today?" Beverly asked.

"You see Angela Bassett's hair in *Waiting to Exhale?*" Gena asked.

"Before or after she cut it off?" Beverly asked.

"After," Gena told her.

"After?" Beverly asked. "Are you sure?"

Gena nodded. "Girl, take it all off. I need a new look."

Beverly shrugged and grabbed her scissors.

"So, where's the Mercedes at, Gena?" Pam asked. "Did you trade it in?"

"No, I still have it," Gena told them.

"Ooooh, girl," Tina wailed. "Mmm," she hummed looking at the others in the room.

Gena smiled. It was none of their business who bought her car. And if she told them that she bought it herself, too many questions would arise. So, she let them believe what they wanted to believe and they wanted to believe that a nigga had bought the car, so let them.

"Girl, I'm so happy to see you doing good," Tracey declared.

Gena exhaled. "Girl, I feel so happy. Jay is a good man."

"You need to bring him to Chances so that we can meet him," Pam told her.

"Girl, he won't go to no club," Gena told her.

"Why, he think he too good or something?" Beverly asked.

"No, he just don't do clubs," Gena told her. "Hell, I really don't do them no more either."

"Oh, you too good to fuck with ya girls now?" Tina asked with a smile.

"Girl, we know you from Richard Allen," Veronica added. "Get your project chick ass out the house and come and kick it with ya girls!"

"You know that if Sahirah was here, she would have your ass out the house," Beverly told her. "Girl, we miss her too. And we miss Qua and Black."

"Yeah, I know, me too," said Gena, thinking about how she and Sahirah used to be in every nightclub every other night of the week.

"Tell that Jay guy to take you to the club, girl," Val told her.

"We'll see," Gena told them. "So is that why all of you ho's is up in here today? Getting ready for the club?"

"Girl, please," Veronica said, waving her off. "The bond hearing is tomorrow."

Gena recoiled. "The bond hearing?"

"Yeah, Rik and everybody's bond hearing is tomorrow," Pam told her.

"Okay, I'm missing something," Gena told them. "What the fuck are y'all talking bout?"

"Girl, Rik, Quinny, Reds, Rasun, Pookey, Amar, Winston, everybody, I mean everybody you can name that we know got busted yesterday," Veronica explained.

"Got busted?" Gena leaned forward in her chair. She was in shock. "Where? How?"

"Girl, the Feds raided all of they asses at the same time, early in the morning the other day," Beverly told her.

"Get the fuck outta here!" Gena shouted.

Veronica nodded sadly.

"What happened?" Gena asked.

"Girl, they got raided by the Feds," Veronica explained.

"They all had indictments. They didn't find anything, but they said that they had been watching them for a while, and that they all had indictments."

Gena shook her head. "Girl, I'm sorry. You should have called."

"Gena, nobody has your number anymore," Bridgette told her. "Girl, we knew that you was doing bad after Qua died, and that you needed some space."

"I'm sorry, I still want to keep in touch though," Gena told them. "I've just been trying to get myself back together. I'm going to give y'all my number before I leave. And, Veronica, I want you to give it to Rik and tell him to call me collect. When are you going to talk to him again?"

"Girl, he's supposed to call me tonight," Veronica told her.

"Give him my number and tell him to put me on his visitation list," Gena told her. "I need to go see him."

Veronica nodded. "I'll tell him tonight."

Gena leaned back in the chair and allowed Beverly to finish up her hair.

"Gena, if that man of yours is doing anything illegal, tell him to get out of the game right now," Bridgette told her. "This shit is not worth it."

Veronica shook her head and wiped the tears out of her eyes. "Yeah, this shit right here is crazy. Everybody's locked up."

Pam handed Veronica a tissue and added, "I just don't understand how they locked up like forty or fifty niggas at one time. That shit is what's crazy to me."

"The problem is too many dudes be snitches!" Beverly

said angrily. "Bitch-ass niggas wanna do the crime, but don't wanna do the time."

"That's right!" Tina shouted, high-fiving Val. "These snitching-ass niggas want to run and get everybody else caught up. Hell, we need to make a new rule. No pussy for snitching-ass niggas!"

"That's right!" Beverly chimed in. "Hell, these niggas don't want to go and do they time, 'cause they want to stay out here and get some pussy and eat McDonald's, and ride around on rims, bumping they systems. Girl, no pussy for the snitches. I don't want no crying, telling-ass nigga up in my shit anyway!"

Veronica wiped her tears again and started smiling. "Thanks y'all. I know y'all trying to make me feel better, and I appreciate it."

"We are, but, girl, we serious too," Beverly told her. "Girl, we putting out a new rule. No pussy if you'se a snitch. Show us your transcripts, your presentence report, your affidavit, and give us three witnesses!"

Laughter shot around the beauty shop.

"Girl, and if they got arrested and ain't never went to trial, that's automatically a bar on the pussy!" Tina added.

"For real!" Beverly wailed. "Nigga, how in the fuck you get busted last year with ten ounces, a machine gun, and two scales in your trunk, and you ain't went to so much as a mutha-fuckin' evidence hearing, let alone a trial!"

Tina pointed to a blank spot on the wall. "Right there is where we need to hang our No Pussy Board! Put the board up, and start putting these niggas' names on it. I betcha they'll cut that bullshit out then."

Beverly handed Gena a hand mirror. "All done, mommy."

Gena rose from the chair and turned and stared into the big mirror on the wall. She used the small mirror to check the back of her hair. Beverly hooked her shit up. She was ready to be in a hair magazine. Gena reached into her purse, pulled out a hundred-dollar bill, and handed it to Beverly along with her phone number, wrapped around the money.

"Keep the change," Gena whispered.

Beverly glanced at the hundred-dollar bill and tucked it away inside the pouch on her apron. Gena walked to Val, who did Markita's hair, and handed her a hundred-dollar bill as well.

"You ready?" Markita asked her.

Gena nodded, gathered her purse, and headed for the door. At the door she turned back toward her friends.

"It was good seeing y'all again," Gena told them. "Veronica, tell Rik to put me on his list."

"Bye, girl," Tina and Veronica said at the same time.

"See ya, Gena." Bridgette waved.

"Bye, y'all. Hey, Tracey, I'll call you later." Gena waved and headed out the door.

Outside, Gena and Markita climbed into her Porsche and pulled away. Again, she did not notice the black Range Rover pulling off into the traffic just behind her.

SKIP TO MY LOU, MY DARLING

Skip unlocked the door to his flat and walked inside. He set his bags of groceries down on the counter and pressed the button on his answering machine to check his messages. No one had called him, and he loved it. He loved his privacy, and his anonymity. It was for those reasons that he had chosen his flat on the industrial side of town, away from the majority of Philadelphia's other denizens. He was surrounded by nothing but a few other flats, numerous industrial buildings, and railroad trucks. His neighbors minded their own business, and no one really cared about what went on in his neighborhood. In fact, nothing really ever did go on in his neighborhood. And even if something did, it was unlikely that anyone would be able to hear it. The constant passing of trains blocked out most noises.

Skip walked to his stove and turned on the front burner. He then walked to his cabinets, opened the door, and pulled out a steel pot. He was hungry, and he had a taste for some oatmeal. Apple-cinnamon-flavored oatmeal, to be exact. He walked to the sink, turned on the faucet, and filled the pot halfway. He then returned to his stove and placed the pot on the lit burner.

Skip was tired. His feet hurt, his bones ached, and he felt fatigue tugging at his entire body. A nice big bowl of oatmeal would certainly seal the deal for him, and give him the full stomach that would put him into a deep all-consuming sleep. It was some sleep that he desperately needed. He couldn't wait to hit the sack.

Skip peered around his flat, seeing what needed to be done. He was a borderline neat freak, so very little was out of place. In fact, if one didn't know better, one would have thought that a woman lived there and kept the place clean. The only thing that needed to be done was to take out the trash. He would do that before he ate, but after he took his medicine.

Skip walked to his refrigerator and opened it. He removed a tiny vial of insulin and an injection needle. He closed the door and made his way over to his dinette set. Skip seated himself at his dining-room table, leaned forward, and rolled up his pants leg. He then tapped his tiny insulin bottle, shaking up the medication, and stuck his needle into the vial. He pulled back the stopper on his syringe until he had drawn in the correct amount of insulin, and then removed the needle and examined the contents. Once he was certain that he had the right amount inside his syringe, he carefully stuck the needle into his thigh and injected the insulin.

His diabetes was something that he had hidden from outsiders for most of his life. He had become a Type 2 diabetic at the age of ten. His body simply failed to produce enough insulin. This insulin deficiency slowly worsened until diet and exercise were no longer enough. And after a few years, even pills were no longer enough. He now found himself a slave to insulin injections, which the doctors said he would need for the rest of his life. The good news, to him, was that his diabetes was well under control. The bad news was that he could never let another member of Junior Mafia find out about it.

That Junior Mafia would kill him if they ever found out was a foregone conclusion. They hated weakness. And to them, he would personify weakness. If he couldn't fight off a sugar cube, how could they trust him to fight off some niggas rolling in on their turf? If word of his condition ever got out, he would be a target not only for Junior Mafia, but for every other dealer in the city who wanted his territory. They would all come after him, thinking him sick and weak. He would have a big fucking M on his forehead, for mark. Easy mark. So he definitely had to keep his condition to himself.

Skip rose from the table, walked to his kitchen trash can, and pulled the bag of trash out. He set the trash bag on the floor, tied it closed, lifted it, and headed for the door. His water was close to boiling, and he would be ready to pour it into a bowl filled with oatmeal and enjoy one of his favorite dishes. His affinity for oatmeal was a product of his youth. He had been raised in the projects on fried bologna sandwiches and big bowls of Frosted Flakes, and equally big bowls of oatmeal had been a staple in his household. If it hadn't been for fried bologna, grits, and Kool Aid, lunch would have been practically nonexistent. And if it hadn't been for cold cereal and oatmeal, breakfast would have been a dream. He still loved all of those things to this day.

Skip lifted the trash bag and headed out the door and around the corner of his house, to where his larger trash cans were kept. He lifted the lid off his large sixty-gallon trash can and tossed his white kitchen trash bag inside. He replaced the lid and made sure that it was on tight, so that the cats wouldn't be able to knock the trash can over and cause the lid to fly off. When this was done, he turned to head back into his house. When he turned, however, he found an unexpected guest.

"Jerrell!" Skip said, surprised. "My nigga! What's happening?"

Skip peered down and saw the black semiautomatic in Jerrell's hand. It was pointed at his stomach.

"Yo, J!" Skip said. "What the fuck's up with the pistol, B?"

Jerrell nodded toward Skip's apartment. "Why don't we go inside and talk about this."

"Yo, this shit is foul, my nigga," Skip told him. "What the fuck kinda shit you playing, yo?"

Skip headed back into his flat, with Jerrell following just behind. Jerrell locked the door just behind himself. Skip turned and faced him.

"Okay, now you wanna tell me what the meaning of this bullshit is?" Skip demanded.

"It's about my money, Skip," Jerrell told him. "All of you niggas fucked off my money!"

"I ain't fucked off shit, nigga!" Skip shouted. "What the fuck are you talking about?"

"Okay then, where's my money for the shit that I fronted you before I got locked up?" Jerrell asked.

"I got your money, nigga!" Skip told him.

Jerrell exhaled. "Don't tell me, you got it, but it's not here. We got to go and get it, right?"

"I got your money right here, nigga," Skip told him.

"Okay, where is it?" Jerrell asked.

"It's inside of that old broke-ass stereo," Skip told him, nodding at an ancient, circa 1980s console stereo. "The speaker cover pops off, and the money is inside."

Jerrell peered at the stereo and then back at Skip. "Get it for me. And no funny business either. And don't try no tricks, no reaching for no pistols, no bullshit, Skip."

Skip walked to the stereo and kneeled down. He popped the cover off the right speaker, reached inside, and pulled out a bundle of money wrapped in plastic. He tossed the bundle onto a chair next to where Jerrell was standing.

Jerrell lifted the money and examined it. There was a light cover of dust on it, telling him that the money had been wrapped up and waiting for him for a good little while. He shifted his gaze to Skip.

"How much is this?" he asked.

"All of it," Skip told him. "Every red cent that I owe you."

Jerrell's mind was fucked up now. He should have known that Skip would have his money. Skip wasn't like the rest of them niggas. Skip was old school. He didn't live lavishly, he didn't try to be flashy, he didn't wear jewelry or drive a fancy car. Skip lived in an old flat next to a train track and drove a banged-up old Jeep Cherokee. Skip had never, not once, come up short with his money. He had always done what he was supposed to do, when he was supposed to do it. He was the most loyal nigga in Junior Mafia. Skip took it seriously. And now, he had shown up at Skip's pad with a pistol and forced him at gunpoint to give him something that he was going to give him anyway.

"Why didn't you come to any of my hearings, or to my

trial, Skip?" Jerrell asked. "Why didn't you show me some love? Why wasn't you there for me when I needed you?"

"What?" Skip asked, surprised. "Nigga, have you bumped your muthafuckin' head or something?"

Jerrell frowned.

"Is that what this bullshit is about?" Skip asked. "You felt like niggas wasn't down for you? You felt like your Mafia family abandoned you? Nigga, I ordered everybody to stay away from all of that shit. Are you crazy?"

"You ordered them to?" Jerrell asked.

"Jerrell! You were facing a conspiracy charge!" Skip shouted. "They wanted you for being the head of Junior Mafia. If you would have had a bunch of Junior Mafia niggas show up to your trial, those jurors would have hung your black ass! We stayed away so that you would have a chance of getting out of that shit! We didn't want to go and visit you in jail 'cause we wanted your black ass out of jail! We stayed away so that you could be free, nigga!"

Jerrell closed his eyes. It was too much for him and he didn't know what to do. Skip was right. And Skip had done the right thing. He was truly a soldier. He had every dime of Jerrell's money and had been waiting for him to come home to give it to him. He had done everything right and had showed Jerrell nothing but loyalty. But Skip's loyalty was to the Junior Mafia, not him, and that brotherhood was dead to Jerrell. All those niggas were a bunch of snakes. They had fucked him over, turned their backs on him, and not one of them tried to slide him a dime when he stepped out.

"You killed them, didn't you?" Skip asked. "You killed our brothers because of this bullshit, didn't you?"

"You don't know what the fuck you're talking about," Jerrell told him, wishing that he'd just stop and not say anything else.

"I do know what the fuck I'm talking about!" Skip yelled. "You killed them, you fucking snake! How could you do that? How could you betray your brothers over something as trivial as money? It's just money, Jerrell. We are your brothers!"

"Brothers!" Jerell shouted. "Brothers? What kind of brothers spend all of their brother's money? What kind of brothers don't give money to their brother's lawyers, or let their brother's family go without? How many of you niggas went to my mom's house and dropped off some bread? How many of you took any money to any of my kids? How hard would it have been to find a dope fiend, give him a twenty, and have him cut my momma's grass for her? You niggas are snakes! You're a bunch of users, riders, muthafuckin' passengers! Well, the free fucking ride is over! It's time to get the fuck off of the Jerrell express! No more muthafuckin' gravy trains here, nigga!"

"Fuck you!" Skip shouted. "When we started this shit, we was all supposed to be equals. You're the one who made yourself into a god. You the one who set yourself up to be the leader over everybody! You did! You stopped being our brother, and tried to be our daddy! You did that shit, nigga! You can't force people to love you like a brother, you have to be a brother. You can't force someone to be loyal, you have to win a nigga's loyalty! I can't believe you killed them."

Jerrell thought quietly for a split second. Skip was right and everything he was saying was right. Skip made perfect sense and Jerrell was doing everything he could to not sway in his decisions. *Do I have to kill Skip? He's been so loyal, but he knows I killed everybody else. He knows that I came here to kill him. I can never trust this nigga again. And I know he'll never trust me, never. Fuck, Skip, why'd you have to have my money? Why'd you have to be right? Damn, I wish I didn't have to, but this nigga just knows too much.*

"Fuck that shit!" Jerrell shouted. "I gave you niggas everything! I took care of y'all. I put you niggas on top! I organized Junior Mafia, I planned the campaigns and the hits to seize those spots, I set up the distribution, I got us the contacts! I took care of everything, and you niggas benefited from it! I showed love, and I got nothing back! I got nothing!"

Skip fell back onto the couch and shook his head. Sweat began to pour from his forehead. "You demanded our loyalty, J. You can't demand a person's loyalty. You wanted to take care of us by handing shit out to us, like it all belonged to you. We all worked hard for that shit. We got out there in those streets, and we killed niggas, and took the risks, took the bullets from taking over those spots. We did it, and we did it together."

Jerrell stood quietly and examined Skip for several moments. "What the fuck's wrong with you, nigga?"

Skip swallowed hard and shook his head. "I just need to eat something, that's all."

"You need to eat something?" Jerrell shifted his gaze toward the kitchen table, where he spied Skip's insulin and syringe. He walked to the table, lifted the bottle, and read the contents. He turned back toward Skip. "Why you lying, conniving, sick muthafucka, you!"

Skip leaned back onto the couch, growing weaker by the moment. His head was pounding and sweat was pouring down his face. "I need something to eat. Some . . . fruit . . . anything. Please . . ."

Jerrell nodded. "I'll give you something, all right. My brother."

Jerrell stuck the needle back into the insulin bottle and pulled the stopper all the way to the top, filling the syringe. He walked to where Skip was now lying on the couch, yanked Skip's shirt up, and stuck the needle into Skip's stomach. He injected the full syringe of insulin into Skip.

"No!" Skip knocked the empty syringe away and tried to get up. He found himself tumbling onto the floor. "Help . . . me . . ."

"Fuck you," Jerrell told him. He stepped over Skip and walked to the stereo, where he pulled the rest of Skip's money out of the speaker.

"Please, you can have all of the money," Skip pleaded weakly. "Just help me. Orange, in the icebox."

Jerrell walked to Skip's other speaker and yanked off the cover. This speaker was packed with blocks of money wrapped in plastic. It had to be millions. He had hit the fucking jackpot.

Skip began convulsing, and foam and slobber began pouring from his mouth.

"So which one is it, Skip?" Jerrell asked, as he removed the money from Skip's speaker. "Are you having a diabetic stroke, a diabetic heart attack, or is it just a really bad reaction? You look pretty bad, Skip. You'll probably have been in a coma for way too long before anyone finds you. And that means, even if you survive, you'll most likely be a vegetable. Sorry, B. But shit happens."

Jerrell rose, stepped over Skip's motionless body, and headed into the kitchen, where he grabbed a trash bag so that he could carry out all of his newfound wealth. By the time he finished loading his car, he realized that Skip had saved every single penny he had gained from hustling. And it was a damn pretty penny. Skip had been over five million strong. Skip's money, combined with the money that he had taken from all of the others, now made him over ten million strong. He was back on top again. Almost as rich as the old Jerrell.

Jerrell loaded the last bag of money into his Range Rover, peered around the quiet, nearly pitch-black neighborhood, and lit up a fat Cuban cigar. He wasn't a daily smoker; in fact, he only lit up on special occasions. Tonight was a special occasion. Jerrell exhaled, blew the smoke into the cool Philly night breeze, and allowed himself a big, wide grin. It felt fucking good to be the king again.

VISITING HOURS

The county jail was a massive concrete structure with long narrow gun-slit-style windows that were covered over with a thick steel wire mesh. The imposing facade gave the entire complex an air of foreboding. That, and the sharp, thick strands of concertina wire that surrounded the entire establishment, caused goose bumps to appear on Gena's arms.

Gena made her way into the building and located the visitation desk. A heavyset guard seated behind the reception desk peered up at her over his glasses.

"May I help you, miss?" the guard asked.

"Yes, I'm here for visitation," Gena told him.

"Inmate's name?" the guard asked.

"Johnson," Gena told him. "His name is Tyrik Johnson."

The guard looked up the name on his list and lifted the telephone.

"Visitation for Johnson, Tyrik, inmate number one-zero-nine-two-five-two." The guard peered back up at Gena. "You have your driver's license, miss?"

Gena lifted her Chanel bag onto the counter and pulled out her wallet. She opened her billfold, pulled out her driver's license, and handed it to the guard. The guard took the license and typed Gena's information into his computer. When he finished typing her information, he handed the license back to her and nodded toward the hall.

"Visitation room's around the corner," he told her. "You know how to get there?"

Gena nodded. "I know where it is."

The guard nodded. "If you get turned around, just follow the signs posted on the walls."

Gena nodded and headed off toward the visitation room. She had been here before to visit two of her ex-boyfriends, and even a couple of her cousins. She knew her way to the room by heart.

"Who are you here to see?" another guard asked, as soon as she walked through the door into the visitation room.

"Tyrik Johnson," Gena told him.

The guard nodded as he checked his list. "All right, in here, you're gonna need a locker and you'll have to remove all your jewelry. Your pockets need to be empty, no gum, and any money you want to carry inside needs to be contained in a plastic see-thru bag. Carry nothing on you through security except your key to your locker, do you understand?"

He talked so fast, had she been a new jack at the whole process, she'da been assed out. She nodded and took the key from the guard. When she was finished signing in, she waited in the sign-in area until the number the guard had given her was called for search; nothing major, a walk through the metal detector, mouth check, and hand scan.

"Take booth number six."

Gena nodded and headed into the visitation room. As she passed the other booths, she could hear babies crying, women shedding tears, other women talking dirty, while others were cursing and shouting at the persons whom they had came to visit. She found her booth, seated herself on the tiny bench seat, and waited.

Tyrik walked into the room wearing a bright orange, county-issued jumpsuit. His hair was still neatly trimmed, as was his goatee. He smiled uncontrollably when he saw Gena seated in the booth. He grabbed the phone and seated himself in the booth opposite Gena.

"Hey, baby girl!" Rik told her.

"Hey, Rik!" Gena said enthusiastically. "Man, I didn't even know you were locked up. You all right?"

"I'm good," Rik told her. "How about you, how have you been?"

"I'm doing good," Gena told him. "Just getting everything back on track."

Rik nodded. "I heard that. I just can't tell you how good it feels to see you again."

"It feels good to see you, too," Gena told him. "So what are they saying?"

Rik shook his head. "They not saying anything good, mama, that's for damn sure. They hitting us with the whole enchilada. Conspiracy to distribute crack cocaine, and conspiracy to carry out a continuing criminal enterprise. They hittin' us with a conspiracy to manufacture crack cocaine too. They definitely tryin' to roof a nigga in this muthafucka. They got a confidential informant and they got tapes, supposed to be a lot of tapes. They ain't saying what they got on the tapes though, or at least not yet."

Gena lowered her head and leaned her head on the palm of her hand. "So what is the lawyer saying?"

"He's saying that it looks pretty bad, you know. What the fuck can he say, Gena? Shit, only thing I know right now is that we might find out something at the discovery hearing. He thinks that we might be able to figure out who the informant is after discovery. I just wish I knew who the snake muthafucka was . . ."

"So what happens then?" Gena asked. "Even if you find out who it is, will that help you?"

Will that help? Will that help? Is she nuts? I'll dead that nigga before anyone can blink or even think of a trial. Will that help? But of course Rik didn't respond like that; he knew the mice were listening in the walls.

"Well, we can discredit the witness, and shit like that," Rik explained. "But other than that who knows . . ."

Gena shook her head again and wiped at her eyes as she pretended to be tired. She didn't want Rik to see her upset at his misfortune.

"Don't you be tripping over me. You be happy, Gena. I'll handle this. You just worry about Gena, you hear me?"

Gena nodded.

"So, what's this I hear about you having a new man?" Rik asked with a smile.

Gena nodded.

"That's good," Rik told her. "I was so happy to hear that. I'm glad that you're finding happiness again, Gena. You deserve to be happy. Quadir would want you to be happy."

"Who told you? Veronica?"

"Yeah, she claim she having my baby, you know?"

"Oh yeah, congratulations, big papa."

"Man, don't congratulate me till the blood test comes back. Shit, I don't know, Gena, I don't know."

"I don't know neither, Rik." Gena looked up and peered into Tyrik's eyes. "I just don't . . ."

"Hey, I know Qua, he was my nigga, for real, all day strong," Rik told her. "That boy loved you more than anyone else in this world. He loved you with everything that he had. You were his whole world, and making you happy was something he wanted to do for you at all times. Trust me, he would want you to be happy."

"Sometimes it's so hard to go on. I miss him so much, Rik. I still lie in my bed and cry for him. We were supposed to be together forever. It's so hard to live life without him."

"Gena, listen to me. You have to go on. You have to keep on going. It's your love for Quadir that keeps him alive. You have to live life for the both of you now. Your happiness is his happiness, your joy is his joy. Qua is a part of you from now on, and you carry him with you wherever you go. Be happy, baby, live life to the fullest for both of you. The world can be a cruel place, full of trickery; it took away the person who you were supposed to spend the rest of your life with. Life tricked you, so I understand how you must still feel and I don't blame you. But you must find a little bit of happiness out here and take whatever good this life allows you to have, and run with it. So you run with it, Gena. Take whatever is given you, make a new life for yourself, and be happy."

"I'll try, Rik, I'll try. What about you, what about bail?"

"Man, that fuckin' judge said two-million-dollar bail and I thought I would die. I knew then I'd sit for a minute."

"Why? I don't understand why you don't post it."

"'Cause the Feds ain't like the state. In the state, if you get a two-million-dollar bond, you have to get a bail bondsman to get you out, and they'll charge you about two hundred grand. In the Feds you put up the bond money, and you get it back when I show up for trial and stuff."

"Oh!" Gena said, surprised. "Well, do you have it to put up?"

Rik shook his head, not answering that question over the phone.

"Do you want it?" Gena asked.

Rik peered into Gena's eyes. "What do you mean, Gena?"

"Don't answer a question with a question, Rik," Gena said nervously. "Do you want the money so that you can get out on bond?"

"Two million dollars?" Rik asked. "Gena, how are you going to get two million dollars?"

"Do you want the money, Rik?" Gena asked again.

"And this new boyfriend of yours is going to just give you two million dollars to give to my lawyers, so that I can get out on bond?"

"Do you want the money?" Gena asked him again.

Rik thought about what Gena was asking. *Do I want the money? What the fuck would that shit look like if she walks up to my lawyers with two million dollars? It'd be a mess and the Feds would be all over my ass if I made that bail. I definitely don't want that.* So far, they had left his baby momma and his houses alone. He really wanted to keep it that way. He wanted them knowing as little as possible about his money, about his family life, about his business. He had to think seriously before he took her up on her offer, and now for the second part of her question.

Rik leaned back against the glass booth and contemplated

Gena's offer. *I do want out of here, bad, but where she even getting this money from? Her new boyfriend? Nah, I ain't buyin' that.* Niggas with that kind of bread to throw around were rare, and he'd know the nigga. The only one he knew personally had been his nigga Quadir. Qua had the paper to do shit like that . . .

Rik dropped his telephone when the thought hit him.

"Rik, are you all right?" Gena asked.

Rik nodded. He was still in shock. *Gena done found Quadir's stash. That explains it all; the new car, the clothes, the jewelry, everything. Why didn't I see that! How could I have been so stupid! Gena's sitting on the most incredible meal tickets, and keeping that shit on the low low.*

"Rik, what's the matter?" Gena asked.

Rik shook his head. "No, nothing, I'm okay."

"So, what's up, baby?" Gena asked. "Do you want to get out on bond or what?"

"Gena, I appreciate the offer, I really do," Rik told her. "But it's a lot more complicated than that. I have to think about what these people will think if I plunk down a two-million-dollar bond."

"It's not your money, so why would they trip with you?" Gena asked.

"Yeah, but they would think that it was my money," Rik explained. "Who would put up two million dollars for someone else? And if they didn't think that it was my money, they would want to know whose money it was, and where they got it from. Do you really want them asking those kinds of questions, Gena? Think about it."

Gena lowered her head and nodded. She knew that he was right.

"I don't want to pull you into this mess, Gena," Rik told her. "I care about you and I would never want you to do anything for me that could hurt you. I want you to stay as far away from this mess as possible. I don't want them looking at you in any way possible, understand?"

Gena nodded. She certainly didn't want that kind of heat. Too many questions would be asked, and they were questions that she definitely wouldn't be able to answer. *Naw, fuck that, Rik is right.*

"Rik," Gena said as she rose from the bench, "you can call me whenever you want, okay?"

Rik nodded and smiled good-bye to her.

Gena placed the phone down on the counter, turned, and walked out of the visitation room with eyes watching her from inside the walls. Something inside her told her that she had just made one of the biggest mistakes of her life. She felt as though she should never have come to this place.

BUGGED OUT

Detective Ellington hit the rewind button on the tape, and once again replayed the conversation during Gena and Rik's visit.

"She is definitely offering him the two million dollars." Detective Dick Davis nodded.

Detective Barrientes nodded. "I agree. It's an offer."

"So, we are all in agreement, that little miss Gena has her dead man's money?" Detective Ratzinger asked.

The detectives arrayed around the room all nodded in agreement.

"So what's our next move?" Detective Barrientes asked.

"We can't grab her, because technically she didn't say that she had the money," Detective Ratzinger told them.

"You think we should squeeze her?" Dick Davis asked.

"Or how about we put twenty-four-hour surveillance on her, until she leads us to the money?" Detective Barrientes offered.

"Maybe we should do both," Detective Ratzinger suggested.

"I have another idea," Detective Ellington told them.

"What's that?" Ratzinger asked.

Letoya Ellington walked to the window and peered out across the downtown skyline. She folded her arms as her thoughts began to formulate. "I say we use our CI on her. They know each other well. Let's get her to confide in him on tape, saying that she has the money, and then we can really squeeze her. We bring her in, I play the big sister role, Davis plays the hammer, and one of us will get it out of her."

Detective Ratzinger nodded. He liked the idea. Besides, getting her on tape was something that they could take to a grand jury if necessary. And they just might do that if she refused to give up the money. They could charge her with money laundering, or profiting from an illicit trade. He would have someone from the DA's office look it up. He knew that living off drug money was illegal, even if you weren't the one that sold the drugs. He was certain that they could find plenty of things to charge her with, and find plenty of statutes under which to seize that money. Again, he nodded his consent.

"Let's run with it, Letoya," Detective Ratzinger told her. "Get your informant up to speed. See what he knows about the money, and about this Gena girl. And then tell him what we need."

Letoya nodded. "He's in the next room. I'll see what I can get out of him."

"Need some help?" Dick Davis asked.

Detective Ellington paused and thought about the offer for several moments. She had already established herself as a hardass with the CI. Maybe she could bring in Dickie Davis to play the good cop.

"Yeah, Dick, maybe I could use a little help," she told him. "Feel up to playing the nice, sympathetic cop today?"

"Why do I always have to play the good guy?" Dick asked, following Letoya out of the room.

"Maybe because you look all nice and sweet and young," Letoya told him. She turned and squeezed Detective Davis's cheek. "And you look seventeen, Dickie. Who's going to be intimidated by someone who looks like the kid who carries out their groceries to the car?"

Detective Ellington strolled into the room where Rasun was seated and waiting for her. Dickie Davis closed the door behind them.

"Rasun, this is Detective Davis, my partner," Letoya told her informant. "Detective Davis, this is the young man who's been helping us out with the investigation."

Detective Davis and Rasun exchanged handshakes.

"So, Rasun, the reason that I had them bring you over today is that I had a few questions for you," Detective Ellington told him.

"I don't think that I want to answer any more of your questions," Rasun told her.

"And why is that?" Detective Ellington asked.

"Because you people are all snakes!" Rasun said venomously.

Detective Ellington laughed at him.

"Why do you say that?" Dickie Davis asked.

"I'm still in jail, ain't I?" Rasun asked. "What the fuck did I do all of this shit for, if I was gonna go to jail anyway!"

"Rasun, we did it to protect you," Detective Ellington explained. "If we had left you on the streets, and rounded up everyone else, then they would have figured out that you've been helping us."

"And what about now?" Rasun asked. "Why am I still in there? Why didn't the judge give me bond?"

"You are bonded out, Rasun," Detective Ellington told him. "You've been released into our custody. We're just waiting for the right time to kick you back out on the street. We are trying to be really careful and make sure that you're safe."

Rasun shook his head. "Man, I don't want to be locked up anymore."

"Okay," Detective Ellington told him. "Some of the others that we arrested are starting to make bond. We'll kick you out with some of them. We'll just say that your attorney got the judge to reduce your bond, and then he posted it and had you released into his custody."

"Will that work, Rasun?" Dickie Davis asked.

Rasun looked down and nodded.

"I have some questions for you, Rasun," Dickie Davis told him. "But before I ask them, I need to know that you're still part of the team. Detective Ellington tells me that you've been a real asset to her investigation, and that they are thinking about going before the United States district attorney and getting you a really sweet deal so that you won't have to go to jail, and so that your mother's house will not be touched. Are you still down for that deal, Rasun?"

Rasun rolled his eyes and nodded as he sat uncomfortably in his chair. Everything about prison was uncomfortable, everything.

"Good, good man," Dickie Davis said, with a pat on the shoulder.

"Did you know Quadir Richards?" Detective Ellington asked him.

Rasun nodded. "Of course."

"How well did you know him?" Dickie Davis asked.

"He was my homie," Rasun admitted.

"How did he die?" Detective Davis asked.

"He was killed in a drive-by outside of a club on New Year's Eve," Rasun told them. "Y'all the police. You should be telling me. Damn, don't y'all know how the fuck he died?"

Letoya nodded. "Okay, we won't insult your intelligence. Was your boy a baller?"

Rasun nodded.

"A big-time baller?" Dickie Davis asked with a smile.

"Is there any other kind?" Rasun asked, looking at Detective Davis like he was stupid.

"So Qua was a baller, huh?" Detective Ellington asked with a smile. "That is what the homies call him, isn't it? Qua?"

Rasun nodded.

"So, Qua must have had some major chips stacked up then?" Detective Davis asked.

Rasun shrugged.

Detective Ellington slapped Rasun's hat off his head. "Did he have some fucking paper or didn't he?"

Rasun jumped and gave Detective Ellington a look that said he wanted to kill her.

"Did he?" Detective Ellington asked again.

"Yeah." Rasun nodded and rubbed his head where she had struck him. "They say Qua was papered up."

"Who is they?" Detective Davis asked.

Rasun shrugged. "Just people, the people on the streets. Qua was known to be papered up. It was just the word on the streets."

"Do you know Gena Scott?" Detective Ellington asked.

Rasun nodded.

"How well do you know her?" Detective Davis asked.

Rasun nodded. "We all right. I talked to her girlfriend, Sahirah, for a minute and I used to see her around and shit."

"Would you consider yourselves friends?" Detective Davis asked.

Rasun nodded. "We cool."

"How well does she trust you?" Detective Davis asked.

Rasun shrugged. "I don't know."

"Would she confide in you?" Detective Ellington asked.

Rasun shrugged. "She was closer to Rik than she was with anybody else. She would confide in him first."

Detective Davis and Ellington shared a glance and made a mental note. She had, after all, just offered Tyrik two million dollars.

"When is the last time you saw her?" Detective Ellington asked.

"Not since Qua's funeral," Rasun told them.

"So, you don't know how she's doing now?" Detective Davis asked.

Rasun shook his head.

"What kind of girl is she?" Detective Davis asked. "I mean, how did she grow up? Was she rich, was she poor? Tell me about her."

Rasun shrugged. "I don't really know nothing about her. She was Qua's girl. I think she grew up over in Richard Allen. I don't think she was papered up or nothing."

"What if I told you that she was rolling in a two-hundred-thousand-dollar Porsche?" Detective Ellington asked.

Rasun shrugged. "Then I would say she doing damn good. Better than I am."

"She kept all of Quadir's money?" Detective Davis asked, leaning in and whispering like he was asking a secret.

Rasun lifted an eyebrow. Damn, it was something that he hadn't thought about. He thought that she was broke.

"You're quiet all of a sudden," Detective Ellington told him. "What's the deal, Rasun? Does she have Quadir's money?"

Rasun shook his head. "I don't know. I mean, the last I heard, old girl was doing bad. Rik was helping her out and shit. Qua's mom pulled a gangster move on her for the house and the cars and shit, booted old girl out on the street with nothing. Everybody thought that the mom and pop had Qua's loochie."

Again, the detectives exchanged glances. This was new information for them. They both tried desperately to make a mental note so that they could later write it all down.

"So, Quadir's mother has his money?" Detective Davis asked.

Rasun nodded. "That's what everybody always thought, because Gena went back to the projects, broke, sad, and all fucked up like the rest of us."

Detective Davis rubbed the lower half of his face and turned away in shock. "So where would she be getting all of her dough from now?" Detective Davis asked.

Rasun shrugged. "Maybe another baller or something. I wouldn't know. I ain't heard nothing about her since after the funeral. Last I heard, she was doing bad, living back at home with her peeps up in the projects."

Detective Ellington opened the door to the interrogation room and nodded for Detective Davis to step outside. Once her colleague joined her in the hall, she closed the door so that Rasun could not hear them talking.

"What the fuck is going on, Letoya?" Detective Davis asked.

"Sounds like we've been attacking this thing from the wrong angle," Detective Ellington told him. "We need to be following the mother, Viola Richards, for that money, and we need to be following Ms. Scott so that we can open up an investigation on her new boyfriend. Sounds like Ms. Gena was accustomed to living a certain way, so she ran out and got her another baller."

Detective Davis laughed. "I still say we see what kind of information he can get out of her. Maybe he can find out who she's messing with, and we can get some good information by putting them two together."

Letoya nodded. "Hell yeah, I still say we wire his ass up and set up a meeting between the two. See what we come up with."

"You take care of the Gena angle, and once we get a name on the boyfriend, I'll start watching him and seeing who he scores from and see if we can put together another major bust."

Detective Ellington lifted her hand into the air, and Detective Davis slapped it.

"Lieutenants by next May!" she declared excitedly.

"Lieutenants by next May!" Detective Davis smiled.

"I'm going to get the paperwork done so that I can cut our bait loose," Detective Ellington said.

"I'll give him the good news and arrange for his transportation back to county in the meantime," Detective Davis told her, while opening the door to the interrogation room.

"Rasun, I got some good news for you!" Detective Davis said excitedly. "You'll be outta this place in a couple of hours, back on your block, hustling your rock just like the good ol' days. Now for the bad news; we need to wire you up again."

Rasun leaned over and began to vomit.

PAYBACK'S A BITCH

Champagne leaped out of her brand-new black S Class 600 wearing a matching black leather cat suit, with matching black leather knee-high boots. The suit looked as though it had been painted onto her body. It was backless, with only her long burnt-orange hair covering her milky yellow skin. She wore an oversized pair of dark Chanel sunglasses and walked as though she was gliding across a catwalk in Paris or Milan. Every man on the street within a two-block radius stopped and stared. Her body was the stuff of every man's fantasy and she knew it; *Buffy who?*

Champagne peered in the direction of the street, and cars came to a screeching halt, with the mostly male drivers all wanting to let her pass so that they could garner a better look at her unrealistic-looking ass. It stuck out so far and was so round that it looked as though you could set a table on top of it. Jerrell sat on the park bench just shaking his head.

"So, this is what you call clandestine?" he asked. "And just in case you don't know what that means, it means secret."

"Fuck you, I know what it means, asshole," Champagne told him.

"You're looking mighty tasty today," Jerrell told her.

Champagne placed her hand on her hip and shifted her weight to one side. "Don't even think about it."

Jerrell smiled. "Not even for old times' sake?"

"Not for all the tea in China, dear heart."

Jerrell pulled out a massive wad of money and tossed it to her. "How about for all of that? Can I hit it for all of that?"

Champagne examined the massive wad of hundreds. "How much is this?"

"See, look at your trick ass!" Jerrell teased. "A minute ago, a nigga couldn't hit for all the tea in China. Now you see cash money and you open like a Chinese takeout spot in the middle of the night, huh?"

"Cream, baby. Gotta get it," Champagne told him.

Jerrell shook his head and snatched his money out of her hand. "I wouldn't stick my dick in you if you gave all this money to me. I might as well go over there and stick my dick in that trash can. It'd be a whole lot cleaner."

Champagne turned and began to walk away. Jerrell leaped up from the bench and clasped her elbow.

"Champagne, wait."

Champagne wiped the tears from her eyes. "What? Let go of me, you sorry son of a bitch!"

"I'm sorry," Jerrell told her.

"I know you sorry," Champagne nodded. "You sorry as hell and I'm tired of your shit. You didn't want me when you had me, so what the fuck you want me to do? Stop living?"

"Champagne, it's just that I still have feelings for you," Jerrell said softly. "And when you said that you wouldn't sleep with me for all the tea in China . . ."

"You have a funny way of showing that you have feelings for someone," she told him.

Jerrell removed her hands from her face and turned her around. "I do. When someone says something to hurt me, the only way I know how to protect myself is to hit back."

Jerrell wrapped his arms around her waist and pulled her close. "What did you find out for me?"

Champagne exhaled. "I found out a lot."

"Oh, really?" Jerrell lifted an eyebrow. "And tell me what exactly 'a lot' is that you found out."

"What do you want to know?" Champagne asked. She unwrapped his arms from around her waist and took a step back from him.

"Does she have a man?" Jerrell asked.

Champagne nodded. "Yeah, you."

A slight smile made its way across Jerrell's face. "Who was her man before me?"

"You mean who was she about to marry," Champagne corrected. "Who was going to be her husband."

"She was in a relationship like that?" Jerrell recoiled slightly from the information.

Champagne nodded. "She was two steps away from marrying Quadir Richards, aka Qua."

"Get the fuck outta here!" he shouted. Jerrell was in shock. His archrival, the nigga whose ground he hated to see himself have to walk on. *Get the fuck outta here. I got Quadir's wife. See, nigga, that's what you get for not getting down with the M.* Damn. Irony was a motherfucker.

Champagne nodded. "Yeah, you fucking Quadir's girl.

Quadir, the nigga that you and your boys killed. Ain't that nothing?" she asked, looking at him out of the corner of her eye like Terry McMillan as she used her fingernail to pick at her teeth.

Jerrell shifted his glance to Champagne. *I can't stand this crazy bitch. Now I know why we didn't make it and why we never will.* Say what you want, but Champagne was quick, and she knew way too much for her own good.

"Is she in the game?" Jerrell asked, getting frustrated.

Champagne shook her head. "The only game she's in is the shopping game. That's all this bitch does is shop and hang out."

"Is she fucking with another baller?" Jerrell asked.

"Besides you?" Champagne asked, lifting an eyebrow. "No."

"And her paper?"

"Where do you think it comes from?" Champagne asked rhetorically. "Umm, let's see, her boyfriend was like one of the biggest dope boys in Philly. They say Quadir was sitting on millions. And that money disappeared the moment they lowered him into the ground. My guess would be it's drug money Quadir left behind. Oops, right answer, Johnny, I win!"

Jerrell turned away from Champagne and thought about what he had just been told. *That nigga Quadir had millions. Word on the street was that the nigga was something like twenty million strong. And if this bitch got his money . . .*

"Goddammit!" Jerrell shouted. "How could I miss this shit? How could I be so stupid!"

"Wha?" Champagne joked, sounding like Amil. "You had a gold mine right beneath your nose all this time, huh? And to think you needed me to figure this shit out for you. I'm not surprised, though."

Jerrell closed his eyes to gather his thoughts. Champagne knew him too well. That left him with one of two options. He could either kill the bitch, or make her his wife. And being that she was much more useful to him alive than dead, he certainly didn't want to kill her. No, he would leave that fate for Ms. Gena. He needed to come up with a plan to get that money from her, and get the hell outta town. Maybe he and Champagne could take all of the money and relocate to the South. A nice crib in Atlanta or Charlotte or Miami sounded real nice right about now; yeah, Miami, or better yet, Palm Beach. He could fuck the shit outta Champagne all night and lay up on the beach all day sipping on exotic-ass drinks; a whole new life. Yeah, he needed new keys.

Jerrell turned toward Champagne. "Thanks for the info, sweetie. I might have an offer for you later."

Champagne lifted an eyebrow. "Oh, really?"

Jerrell smiled and nodded. He leaned forward and kissed her on her cheek. "Yeah. But right now, I got a lot of planning to do."

"I'll bet you do." Champagne smiled.

Jerrell and Champagne shared a knowing laugh. They both knew what he had on his mind. They both knew that he was about to go and sit down somewhere and make preparations to rob a bitch. Oh, what fate lay ahead was unknown, but one thing was for certain, ol' Mr. Jerrell would be planning to come out on top.

*   *   *

Bria lifted Gah Git's coffee cup off the table, walked to the coffee pot, and refilled it. "Gah Git, you want some milk in here?"

Gah Git nodded. "Yeah, baby. And put a little sugar in there for me too."

Brianna walked through the kitchen with a load of laundry in her arms, heading for the utility room where the washing machine was kept.

Bria placed Gah Git's coffee on the table and then grabbed the trash bag out of the garbage can and headed out the back door.

"Gena still ain't called?"

"No, ma'am," said Brianna.

"It's been over a week, and she ain't even called me."

"She all right, Gah Git. My girlfriend's sister works at the hairdresser and she was in there getting her hair done. Don't worry, she just mad at us right now. She'll be back."

"I sure do hope she okay out there in them streets. Mad or not, she could call me and talk to me, let me know she's okay."

Just then they all three heard the sound of the doorbell, and seconds later as Bria opened the door, Gah Git and the twins heard Khaleer shouting. "It's Uncle Michael. Uncle Michael's here," he said as he ran back into the kitchen to tell Gah Git.

Gah Git jumped up and almost pushed Bria down trying to get past her and get to the door.

"Michael," she said, flinging the door back to see her baby boy standing there.

"Ma," he said, before falling into her arms just like he used to do when he was a baby.

"Dag, Uncle Michael look good," whispered Bria.

"He sure do. He lucky he's our uncle," agreed Brianna.

Gena rolled over and looked at the alarm clock on the night-stand on the other side of the bed where Jerrell was still sleep-ing. She rolled back over and lay in the bed thinking about the past couple of weeks. She had finally found an apartment, off City Line Avenue on the Philadelphia side. A nice apartment right in back of Friday's restaurant. She had a security gate, so no one could just get into her complex, and she had an alarm system inside her apartment, so she felt safe there. She was assigned two parking spaces for her cars and she was allowed to have dogs and cats for an additional security deposit. The kitchen was small, but had an eat-in, a dining room, fam-ily room, master bed, master bath, and one half bath. It was honestly all she needed for herself. She had central air, wall-to-wall carpeting, washer, dryer, garbage disposal, white cabi-nets with green granite countertops, and she had the nerve to have imported tile set in the floors and half of the walls in the master bath. It was quite charming and affordable. Gena was scheduled to pick up the keys next week. She had been to every furniture store in the city from the ones up on the boulevard down to the ones in South Philly, and had furnish-ings paid for and ready to be delivered. She was excited, to say the least. This would really be her own apartment. The apartment that she once had was a three-story row house that her uncle Michael owned in West Philly on Chancellor Street next door to her girlfriend Markita. She thought the whole time she was there that he paid her rent, but the truth was there wasn't any rent because he owned the building.

She looked over at Jerrell sleeping. He had been really nice about letting her stay with him. She could tell that he didn't really want to in the beginning and he certainly never gave her a key, so in her heart of hearts she knew her stay with him was temporary, but it was nice playing house the few weeks she was there. Jerrell, unbeknownst to her, was very domesticated, believe it or not. He cooked, he cleaned, he ironed, he pretty much did it all, even grocery shopped and seemed to know the grocery store like the back of his hand, locating everything from soap to paper towels with ease. He certainly didn't need a woman to keep it together for him. He was meticulous, neat, and kept his apartment in tip-top shape. While he had a cleaning service once a week to come in to do the major cleaning, he did a fine job keeping his place tidy. Every morning when they got up, he'd cook breakfast, and sometimes even dinner. And he didn't make simple dishes either, he made stuff that she didn't know how to cook, like grilled salmon with curry mango chutney sauce, green beans with wild mushroom casserole. And one night he even had pot roast so tender the meat fell off the fork. She was quite impressed with him and had no idea he was so independent. But Jerrell had learned early in his life to never depend on a woman for anything, and that's how he sustained himself so well, being single. All he pretty much needed a female for was pussy; other than that, he needed women for nothing at all.

Jerrell rolled over and saw Gena lying in the bed staring up at the ceiling.

"Whatcha doing?" he asked as he pulled her closer to him and snuggled with her.

"Nothing really, just thinking."

"About what?"

"My new place."

"Oh, you ready to roll out, huh?"

"Don't even try it. You know you're ready for me to go," Gena said, tickling his underarm.

Naw, bitch, I don't want you to go nowhere with all that paper you holding. You got this shit twisted. If you holdin' like I think you are, you can stay here as long as you want.

"Man, you must be crazy. I don't want to stop you from doing you, you know what I mean, but you more than welcome here, ma. Please believe it."

"As good as you cook, it's gonna be hard to go."

"Sure it don't have nothing to do with Big Daddy Candy Cane here?" he said, motioning toward his penis.

"Um, you know, now that I think about, I might not be able to ever leave your side."

"See, now you saying something."

"Whatever. You gonna make breakfast?" she asked, now accustomed to his breakfast-in-bed routine.

"Yeah, what you want?"

"Waffles and turkey bacon, scrambled eggs with cheese, and some fresh-squeezed orange juice, please."

"Look, you putting me to work as it is."

"You'll be all right."

Jerrell cooked breakfast and cleaned up his kitchen before Gena had finished showering and getting dressed. The two ate together and then discussed their day and evening plans. Jerrell read the paper, while Gena watched Jerry Springer.

"Do you believe these people?"

"I believe anything. There's nothing that surprises me, Gena."

Gena thought about surprises and her family secret that everyone seemed to know except her. She sort of felt bad because she hadn't called Gah Git since and she knew that Gah Git was probably worried to death about her. *Maybe I'll go see her today,* Gena thought, wondering if that was a good idea.

She got up from the table and started grabbing her essentials to get out the door: sunglasses, pocketbook, and cell phone.

"Hey, Jay, you seen my car keys?"

"Yeah, on the counter in the glass dish," he said, pointing at them.

"Damn, what would I do without you?"

"Be all fucked up," he said. *No, the question is where will I be with that money you holding once I get it.*

Gena grabbed her keys, bent over and kissed Jerrell good-bye, never having a clue that his saving her day back at the gas station was only a ploy to follow her closely. His whole objective was to find where she was keeping her money and then rob her ass. But, she had yet to lead him to her hiding place. *I hate to see you go, but I'll be following you, don't you worry.*

"Have a good day," he hollered as she closed the door, waving good-bye.

Gena drove up Broad Street. She was headed to meet her cousin Gary, who had finally returned her call. She turned off Broad and drove a few blocks over to Camac Street. Gary was outside, just as he said he would be, sitting on his front porch. Gena parked her car and made her way over to Gary.

"Hey, hey, hey!" He motioned to her.

"Hey to you too," Gena said, giving him a hug.

"Hey, cuz!" Gary said, spinning her around. "How have you been?"

"Going crazy without you!" Gena told him. "Boy, you don't know how to call nobody!"

Gary shook his head and smiled. "Man, you just don't know how busy I've been, plus I lost my phone, so I got your messages but you didn't leave me no number and I didn't have it 'cause it wasn't in my phone and then by the time I seen Gah Git, it was like damn near a month had gone by. I'm sorry."

Gena grabbed Gary's hand and led him away from the front porch. "You can tell me all about it while we walk and talk."

Gary shrugged as Gena led him down the street. "Really nothing to tell. Just working."

"And how is domestic life?" Gena asked. "Living with that new girlfriend of yours. Are you two getting along?"

Gary laughed and nodded. "About fifty percent of the time, which is pretty good, I hear. We argue over the most trivial shit you can imagine, though. But other than that, it's all right. And how about you? I hear you got a new man?"

Gena smiled and shrugged. "He's all right. He's good to me, treats me nice."

"Do you love him?" Gary asked.

Gena crinkled up her nose as she contemplated that question. She had never really sat down and thought about it. She had never looked at herself in the mirror and seriously asked that question. *Do I love Jay?*

"I don't know. I don't know."

Gena really didn't know if she could even see herself living with this man for the rest of her life. Strangely, her mind drew a blank on the answer to that question. It was then when she realized how little she actually knew about her new man of life. How could she be prepared to spend the rest of her life with a man whom she knew so little about? She hadn't met any of his family, she knew none of his friends, and she didn't know anything about his past. *Maybe I need to put Mr. Jay under investigation.*

"Your silence answered my question," Gary told her.

"I was just thinking real hard about it," Gena told him.

"If it takes you that long to think about it, then the answer is obviously no." Gary stopped in the middle of the street and turned to her. "Hey, cuz. There's no rush. Don't think that you are in a race, or that you have to run out there and find somebody to replace Quadir, because you don't. Take your time, and love will come. It'll come when you least expect it."

"Enough about love. All I really want to know is, why you ain't tell me?" she asked him, not wanting to believe he knew too.

"Tell you what, about your moms? Come on, man, you charging me? Gena, my moms ain't having it. That shit is old news, like back when it all went down."

"What went down?"

Gary looked at his cousin and honestly he didn't know what to do. He knew if he went against what his mom had said he could have a true family life crisis to deal with.

Stay out of it. Gena's father needs to explain, he needs to tell her what happened to her mother. That was Paula's voice and opinion he heard in his head. So he never spoke about it and he didn't want to now.

"You know I love you, right? So, when I tell you this, don't get mad and don't say that I told you, okay?"

"Gary, come on, I'm not going to tell nothing and I would never put your name in nothing. You know that," she said, pleading to know what seemed like the biggest secret in the world.

"Okay, check this out, right, your mom and Uncle Malcolm was together for like a real long time, right? But, all the while . . ."

"All the while what?" Gena asked, upset that he stopped conversing in the middle of a sentence like that. "Come on, tell me, what?"

"All the while she was married to Uncle Malcolm, she was sleeping with Uncle Michael, and one day your dad came home and caught them together . . . and he . . . shot up Uncle Michael and then strangled your mother."

"My dad killed my mother?"

"Yeah, true story, and Uncle Michael lived and even though he didn't testify, Uncle Malcolm still went to prison for killing your mother. They say you witnessed it, but you was little, like two or three or something."

Gary knew there was more to the secret, much more, but this was where he drew the line, and this was all that he was going to tell her. They headed back to the porch and sat down.

"Please, Gena, you can't say I told you this, all right? I swear I don't want to hear my mother's mouth."

Gena just sat there staring into the thin fall air, not really looking at anything in particular. There was a breeze blowing up on Gary's porch and the two of them sat there for the next hour and seventeen minutes not saying one word. The sounds of the city and cries of the streets filled the air, but Gena blocked it all out. She took in every word that Gary spoke. *How could they keep something like that a secret all this time? My father killed my mother and I watched him do it. I don't remember that, I don't remember that at all.* Gena pierced the inner depths of her brain trying to recollect and couldn't fine one iota of a thought that brought any memory of that fateful day. She had always wished she had her mother, always wished for her in her life. She had needed her mother all her life, and to find out why she couldn't have her was heartbreaking. She didn't know what or how to feel about her father. She had always wanted him too. All her life she wished that he wasn't locked away so that they could have been together, but now, she was older. She had her own life going on and she rarely even thought of him. But she would now.

The breezes that quietly blew had seemed to begin to blow a little harder with every word Gary spoke. And the smooth breeze that once blew across her face now seemed to turn to winds that whipped across her face; stinging, violent, danger-ous even. They were wild winds, winds of uncertainty. She was playing her life by ear at the moment, with no certainty of anything, and that was becoming more and more uncom-fortable to her. Her family and everything she knew her life to be had been suddenly unbalanced, and she felt somewhat un-sure and inadequate and very vulnerable. Then there was Jay, and she honestly didn't know what the relationship they were sharing was all about. She just didn't know enough about him to make any solid decisions. Yes, the breeze was a strong wind, and it smacked her in the face. She needed a plan, she needed stability, she needed to know where she and Jay really stood, and what her feelings toward him really were. And now a man who had been a stranger to her seemed to be the most familiar thought of all. All the dilemmas of her life had seemed to fall in her lap at once. She felt sick, almost ready to vomit, and after every word Gary had said, the sick feeling seemed to increase. She reached down and rubbed her belly, hoping her hand motion would soothe her stomach. Unknown to her, her sickness had nothing to do with Gary, her father, or her mother. Her upset stomach was from the small life she was carrying, the small life that would change her entire world.

SCHEMSTERS

O'Hara's was an old smoke-filled establishment located in the city's old section. The Irish-themed bar played host primarily to the city's working-class plebes. Construction workers, firefighters, emergency medical services technicians, and policemen all congregated within the four walls of the dimly lit establishment. Conversations ranging from the blood and gore of patching up bullet wounds to the proper techniques for putting out smoldering brush could be heard throughout the establishment. Off-duty police officers bragged about their marksmanship skills, while others simply drowned their troubles silently in glass after glass of Scotch. Gathered around one of the old wooden circular tables was a group of Philly's finest that had celebrated themselves into an inebriated state.

Lieutenant Ratzinger lifted his glass in a toast. "To Letoya Ellington, one of the best damn detectives it's been my sorry misfortune to meet!"

"Hear, hear!" Dickie Davis shouted, while lifting his glass into the air.

"To Letoya Ellington, the most meticulous, the most crawl-up-your-ass, leave-no-stone-unturned detective a guy has ever met!" Detective Cornell Cleaver added.

The detectives around the table broke into laughter.

"You deserved that promotion, Toya," Lieutenant Ratzinger told her. "You did a standup job on that investigation. You handled that CI perfectly, you coordinated the raids, and you managed the entire operation with perfection. I wish we had a dozen more like you on the force."

Detective Ellington lifted her glass into the air. "Thanks, guys. You guys are absolutely the best. A girl couldn't ask for a better partner, a better ex-partner, and a better boss. You guys are the best."

"We're the best!" Detective Cornell Cleaver shouted.

"To Philly's finest!" Dickie Davis shouted.

Dozens of firemen and police officers began cheering.

Detective Davis rose from the table, swaying back and forth in a drunken stupor. "Ladies and gentlemen, may I have your attention, please! May I have everyone's attention?"

Slowly, the bar grew silent, and all eyes shifted their focus to the detective.

"I have an announcement to make," Detective Davis continued. "I have with me one of Philadelphia's finest detectives. She is a phenomenal woman, and the best partner that a guy could ask for. She's the best woman I know with a Glock and she can drink and piss fire with the best of them."

Laughter shot through the bar.

"Today, my partner was promoted to the rank of sergeant, which was a promotion that was long overdue," Dickie Davis slurred. "She's saved my ass so many times that I've lost count. She lays it on the line every day, to make the streets safe for all of us. And if she wasn't such a mean-ass motherfucker, and if I wasn't scared of her, I would marry her."

Laughter shot through the bar again.

"Ladies and gentlemen, my partner, the newly promoted Sergeant Letoya Ellington!"

Cheers shot throughout the establishment, while everyone stood and clapped, giving Letoya Ellington a standing ovation. Letoya stood and lifted her glass in acknowledgment.

"A round on the house for Letoya," the bartender shouted. "But one round only, you lousy meatheads. I catch anybody trying to double back, I'm busting chops!"

The officers inside the establishment really began shouting and cheering. This was truly their establishment, as the bartender, Stuckey, was one of their own. Stuckey had retired from the force as a captain, and opened the bar up several years ago. He had made it a home away from home for Philadelphia's law enforcement personnel. The bar was filled with plaques and citations that he had been awarded, as well as lots of other police and firefighter memorabilia. It also had decommissioned weapons hanging on the walls, as well as lots of Texas Ranger memorabilia. Stuckey had a deep affection for the legendary Rangers, as well as for other well-known lawmen of the Old West. Old western badges and wanted posters and pictures hung throughout the establishment. The bar was truly a law enforcement officers' haven.

Dickie Davis reseated himself and turned toward his partner. "Congratulations, Toya. I'm so proud of you."

"Thanks, Dick," Letoya told him.

"Hey, pull it out," Dickie told her. "Let me take a look at that thing!"

Letoya smiled, reached into her purse, pulled out her shiny new gold-colored sergeant's badge, and showed it to her partner.

Lieutenant Ratzinger took the badge and examined it. "I remember the day I made sergeant. It was one of the proudest moments in my life. I think it was three days after that when I got my divorce papers, which was an even happier moment."

The detectives arrayed around the table broke into laughter.

"How it always is," Detective Cleaver told them. "We work our butts off, and we pay the price for it at home."

"We miss the school plays, the anniversaries, the PTA meetings, the birthday parties . . ." Dickie Davis continued.

"And we get served with the divorce papers, while they just keep on getting richer," Ratzinger added.

"Straight bullshit!" Detective Ellington declared.

"I busted a punk the other day who had twenty thousand dollars on him," Detective Cleaver told them. "Right in his front pockets! The kid had twenty thousand dollars in pocket change, half my fucking annual salary, right inside his pockets."

"I busted a kid last week who had a Range Rover for every day of the week," Ratzinger told them. "A fucking different-colored Range Rover for each day of the week. And the kid's house looked like one of those houses on the cover of *Rich and Famous* magazine! The kid had fucking marble floors all throughout the place. Marble! And not the bullshit that you find just anywhere, no, this was the good shit."

"They ride around like they just won the lottery, while we're risking our lives living paycheck to paycheck," Dickie Davis said, shaking his head. "I drive a Toyota, they drive Porsches and Mercedeses."

"Sometimes it kinda makes you feel like you're on the wrong team," Ratzinger told them.

"Yeah, because the law protects them more than it does us," Cleaver added. "And we're the good guys. Shouldn't the good guys be the ones not having to scrape by?"

"They should." Ratzinger nodded. "They really should. The playing field sucks."

"Well, maybe it's time that the playing field was equalized, dammit!" Detective Cleaver declared.

"What do you mean?" Dickie Davis asked.

"Maybe it's time that the good guys took what they deserved!" Cleaver told them.

"How?" Detective Ellington asked. "Busting up some drug ring, so the Feds can come in and seize all of the assets, and then pass us the leftovers?"

"Who says we need the Feds!" Ratzinger declared. "I'm tired of their bullshit anyway."

"You mean start keeping the funds for the department?" Detective Ellington shook her head. "Feds won't go for that one!"

"Who said that the Feds even have to know?" Ratzinger asked them. "Hell, who said that the department even has to know?"

"What are you suggesting, Lieutenant?" Dickie Davis asked.

"I'm saying there is about fifteen million dollars in unaccounted drug money, belonging to a dead drug dealer, that's waiting to be found," Ratzinger told them. "Nobody knows about it, nobody is going to miss it. And I for one would rather see that money in the hands of some hard-working police officers who lay their lives on the line every day than see it in the hands of some young bimbo whose only claim to it is letting some fucking low-life scumbucket drug dealer fuck her in the ass."

"So, let me get this straight," Detective Davis said. "Are you saying that we keep this money, if we find it?"

Detective Cleaver placed his arm around Dickie's shoulder. "That's exactly what he's saying, my boy; we'd be setting up our own little private retirement fund."

"We do all of the work, and we track down that money and find it, why shouldn't we keep it?" Ratzinger asked.

The detectives around the table nodded in agreement.

"Are we all in?" Detective Cleaver asked.

"I'm in," Ratzinger announced.

Dickie Davis nodded. "I'm in."

"Sergeant?" Detective Cleaver asked.

Sergeant Ellington stared off into space and thought about the consequences of her answer. These were her fellow officers seated around the table. Guys who she trusted, guys who trusted her. They had her back, unquestionably, and now they were asking her to do something that was definitely not fully legal.

Letoya leaned back in her seat and thought about what they were asking of her. The money was illegal proceeds from the sale of narcotics. And it did belong to a dead drug dealer. And nobody would really miss it, because nobody even knew that it existed. Nobody except for this drug dealer's mother, or his widow, and neither one of them deserved to keep that money. They couldn't go to the police and say hey, the police stole my illegal drug money, could they? And she and her brother detectives did lay it on the line each and every day for nothing. Hell, her lights came close to getting cut off last month! They could take that money and pay off their bills, and use the rest of it to help get things done. They could use it as flash money, or buy money, without having to go to the department and fill out ten thousand request forms. That money could actually be used for some good.

"Letoya, are you in?" Dickie Davis asked.

Letoya Ellington looked at her partner's face and realized how badly he wanted her to be down with him. She knew that Dickie desperately needed that money. He was the only child of a pair of rapidly aging parents, who had little money and rapidly escalating medical expenses. She couldn't let her partner down.

"Of course, I'm with you guys," she declared.

The group leaned in closer around the table and began to speak in hushed tones.

"This doesn't leave this table, agreed?" Ratzinger declared.

"Agreed," Detective Cleaver said.

"Agreed." Dickie Davis nodded.

"Affirmative," Letoya agreed.

"We lean on the broad, and on the mother, and we find that cash," Ratzinger whispered. "We get the cash, we threaten whoever had it with prosecution and a long jail term, and we hush them up. We split the cash four ways, and we never speak of it again. And remember, nobody puts the cash in a bank, and nobody splurges on anything crazy. We don't need Internal Affairs all over our asses. Is that clear?"

"Clear." Dickie Davis nodded.

"I'm Internal Affairs," Detective Cleaver told them. "I'll cover our asses from that end and keep my eyes and ears open."

"Agreed," Letoya told them.

"One question," Dickie Davis said.

"What's that?" Lieutenant Ratzinger asked.

"What if the mother or the girlfriend or whoever doesn't want to keep silent after we snatch the money?" Dickie asked.

"Then we silence them," Cleaver told them. "Are we all in agreement on that? We do this, we go all the way if necessary. Is that clear? We are all in, all the way!"

Detective Davis nodded. He had never shot anyone before. In fact, he had never even fired his gun, not even in the line of duty. And now they were potentially talking about murdering someone for money. He wondered if he had gotten in over his head.

"All in," Letoya declared.

Lieutenant Ratzinger nodded. "We go all the way, guys. We have to lay somebody down, we do it. No turning back. It's payday for the good guys."

"Payday, for the good guys," Dickie Davis repeated, lifting his glass into the air.

"Payday," Letoya said, lifting her glass.

"It's about fucking time," Detective Cleaver declared, lifting his glass. He would kill for thousands, he thought to himself. For millions, he would bury every fucking nigger in Richard Allen and then bulldoze that motherfucker personally.

HOME SWEET HOME

Gena stepped into the freshly painted apartment and inhaled deeply. She loved the smell of new construction. She didn't know whether it was the smell of new carpet, the smell of the fresh paint, or the smell of the fresh lumber hiding behind the walls. Whatever it was, it was a smell that she adored.

Gena walked further into the apartment and spun around, taking in the apartment's many features. The small brass chandelier over the dining area, the massive brick fireplace in the corner of the family room, the nice light eucalyptus-colored wood cabinets in the large kitchen, the sparkling granite countertops, the white-painted crown molding and baseboards throughout the apartment, and the view of downtown were all of the things that her mind was trying to rapidly absorb. Yes, this was definitely it. After days and days of morning sickness and thinking that she merely had some type of stomach virus, Gena had gone to the doctor and learned that she was pregnant. She was excited, or happy, rather, scared and unsure of what to do. She decided to get a three-bedroom instead of a one-bedroom, so if she needed extra space, she'd be prepared.

"The apartment has twenty-two hundred square feet. The master bedroom and the two secondary bedrooms are all up-stairs," the leasing agent told her. "The master has its own bathroom, and the two secondary bedrooms share a bath-room. There is also a half bathroom here on the first floor. The apartment comes with all stainless-steel appliances, in-cluding a built-in dishwasher and refrigerator. Of course you have your fireplace, and your bar, and you also have your own utility room."

"Gena, girl, this place is banging," Tracey told her.

"You have a nice dining area, and plenty of built-in shelves as well as closet space," the leasing agent announced. "And se-curity here is first rate. The complex is completely gated, and there is a guard at the entrance, so everyone checks in before being allowed to enter onto the premises—but you know all that already from your tour of the one-bedrooms."

"Oh, girl, they got security at the gate!" Tracey laughed. "That'll keep all the bustas out."

"There is an on-site indoor gym, an indoor and an out-door swimming pool, two basketball courts, a playground for children, a sand volleyball court, covered parking spaces for the residents, and residents' clubhouse, complete with seating, a big-screen television, video games, card tables, air hockey table, pool tables, and the works," the leasing agent told them. "And there is residents' night on Fridays, when the residents of the complex get together and watch newly released movies in the gathering center."

"Girl, sounds like we done died and gone to heaven! I wish I could live here." Tracey laughed.

Gena continued to examine the apartment. She thought about the furnishings that she was ready to have delivered and how nice they would look in the apartment.

"Girl, what are you thinking?" Tracey asked.

"About where to put my aquarium filled with sharks." Gena smiled.

"An aquarium? Filled with sharks?" Tracey asked.

The leasing agent laughed.

"Sharks?" Tracey asked again.

Gena nodded. "The small ones. The ones that don't get real big."

"Let's go look upstairs, girl!" Tracey said excitedly. "Some damn sharks! Girl, you crazy!"

Gena turned and followed her friend up the stairs into the landing area.

"This area is really large," the leasing agent pointed out. "It would make a really nice upstairs game room. You could put a nice size television against that wall, and a sofa and love seat over here. You could do this room really nice. And there's a phone outlet up here, and a cable outlet as well."

Tracey made her way into the master bedroom. She screamed.

"Girl, what's the matter?" Gena asked, rushing to see what the deal was.

"Girl, this damn bedroom is bigger than my whole damn apartment!" Tracey told her.

"Bitch, you scared the shit out of me!" Gena told her.

Tracey opened up the master closet. "Girl, this is my bedroom right here. Your closet is my bedroom."

Gena peeked into the closet. She knew that she was going to have a lot of fun filling that closet up with shoes and clothes.

Tracey rushed to the master bathroom and threw open the double doors. "Girl, there is a Jacuzzi in here big enough for two people!"

Gena smiled. Thoughts of her and Jay snuggling up in the tub made her feel warm inside. She could imagine herself riding him in the tub, until she thought of her new passenger and a big, round, protruding stomach, and the thought of riding Jay somehow seemed to disappear.

"Girl, I don't know," Tracey told her. "This place might be a little too big for you all by yourself!"

"Not really," Gena told her.

"Girl, what are you going to do with all of this room?" Tracey asked.

"You can turn one of the bedrooms into a study," the leasing agent suggested.

"I don't know, it just seems so big for you, Gena. You sure you need all this space? It's just you living by yourself, remember. Girl, I'd be scared up in this chumpy all by myself."

"This was nothing compared to the house I lived in with Quadir. Girl, this is a little small for me."

"You won't be scared?"

"Mmm-mmm."

"Lonely?"

"Mmm-mmm."

"All right, then, go ahead and do the damn thing, but this place sure is big."

"Tracey, wouldn't this room look really nice in pink?" Gena asked.

Slowly she peered around the room. "I guess so . . ."

"I could put the crib on that wall and a dresser here and a changing table over there. What do you think?"

Tracey looked at her friend sideways. "Gena, you pregnant."

"Am I?"

Tracey gasped. Once the initial shock wore off, she grabbed Gena and began screaming. "You! Oh, my god! Why didn't you tell me? Oh, my god, Gena, you're pregnant! We're going to have a baby!"

Tracey screamed at the top of her lungs. Gena laughed and kept pushing her off.

"Congratulations," the leasing agent said with a wide smile.

"No wonder you need this great big old place!" Tracey figured. "What did Jay say when he found out?"

"He doesn't know yet," Gena confessed.

"He doesn't know!" Tracey shouted. "Oh, my god, Gena! Why haven't you told him?"

"I just found out myself," Gena lied, not sure why she hadn't said a word. "Besides, I'm not really sure. I took the test, and it came out really light. And then the second one said that I was pregnant. And then the third one said that I was pregnant."

"Then, bitch, you pregnant!" Tracey told her. "Girl, get your ass to the doctor!"

"I'ma go. I got an appointment with a Dr. Afriye Amerson," Gena told her.

"You want me to go with you?" Tracey asked.

"You can, if you want to," Gena said.

"So, when are you going to tell Jay?"

Gena shrugged. "Girl, I don't know. I guess when I feel like the time is right."

"You know he gonna be trying to move up in here with you and the baby," Tracey told her. "See, I didn't know that you was pregnant. But that changes everything."

"Maybe, maybe not," Gena declared.

"How many months are you?" Tracey asked.

"Girl, I'm weeks, only a few weeks at that. I just missed my period. But I can feel it already."

"Then how do you know it's a girl?" Tracey asked. "You getting me all excited and you don't even know for sure!"

"Girl, I can feel it," Gena told her. "I think it's a girl."

Tracey put her hands on her hips and eyeballed Gena. She just couldn't believe it.

"So what do you think?" the leasing agent asked, as she strolled back into the room.

Gena peered around the apartment and nodded. "I like it."

"How are the schools around here?" Tracey asked.

The leasing agent laughed. "Well, she won't be worried about that for a while. But just to let you know, I think the school system in this neighborhood is the best. My own son goes to school in this district."

"How far are you going to be commuting from work?" the agent asked Gena.

Gena shook her head. "I won't have to commute. I'm self-employed. I'll be working out of the apartment basically."

"Oh, really?" The agent smiled. "What do you do?"

"I'm a talent agent," Gena lied.

"Oh, how interesting!" the agent declared. "Do you represent anyone I know?"

"Probably." Gena smiled and quickly changed the conversation. "So, what's the next step here?"

"Well, your credit application was already approved for the one-bedroom, so I'll just need an additional security deposit and your signature on the lease, and we can take care of that right now, if you like."

"Okay, then, let's do it," Gena said, ready to sign her name on the dotted line as her phone began to ring. She scrambled through her bag and spoke into the receiver.

"Hello?"

"Hey, Gena, what's going down?" Rasun asked.

"Who is this?" Gena asked, not certain who the voice on the other side of the phone belonged to. It sounded familiar, really familiar, but she couldn't make it out.

"It's me, Rasun."

"Hey!" Gena said, becoming animated. "What have you been up to! Wow, it's been a long time!"

"Yeah, I know," Rasun told her. "Hey, I really need to talk to you."

"Oh, yeah?" Gena asked. "What's up?"

"I really don't want to talk about it over the phone," Rasun told her. "Is there any way I can meet you somewhere?"

"Yeah, sure, " Gena answered. "When?"

"How about tomorrow?" Rasun asked. "Hey, meet me at that spot where we used to count dough."

Gena thought about it for several moments until she remembered. It was a motel on the edge of town. Qua had taken her there before when he had gone to count up some money with the boys.

"What time?" Gena asked him.

"How about seven?" Rasun asked.

"See you tomorrow at seven," Gena told him. She disconnected the call. Thoughts ran through her head about the strange call that she had received. She wondered what it could be that he wanted.

Rasun hung up the telephone and leaned his head against it. He didn't want to do this. He felt as if he were betraying a friend. Quadir had been there for him when no one else had, and he hated having to set up his girl. But it was his freedom, his mother's freedom, and his mother's house on the line. Quadir would just have to understand, and if not, then fuck him.

Rasun lifted his head, turned, and headed for his car. He climbed inside, cranked up the stereo, and pulled off. He didn't pay attention to the black BMW pulling off just behind him.

SNEAKY SNEAKY

Jerrell walked through the hardware store like a kid in a candy store. He turned his basket down the first aisle and grabbed a long cord of thick yellow rope. He tugged at the plastic rope, testing its strength. Once he was satisfied that it would hold, he placed it inside his basket and headed for the next item on his list.

Jerrell turned onto the aisle with the duct tape and tossed a couple of rolls into his shopping cart. He headed over to the aisle where the chains were kept. He reeled off about ten feet of thick, stainless-steel chain and had one of the store's customer service personnel cut it for him. The chain was heavy, just what was needed for the job that he had in store for it.

In the home and garden section, Jerrell selected two large metal buckets, and two bags of quick-dry cement. He loaded his wares into the basket and headed over to the checkout counter.

"Somebody's doing some home improvement," the salesgirl joked as she gave him a flirtatious smile.

"You just don't know how much this project is going to pay off," Jerrell answered back.

"They say that the best way to increase value is by sprucing up the kitchen and bathrooms!" the salesgirl advised him.

Jerrell nodded and smiled. "Oh, yeah, this is definitely going to increase my net worth significantly."

"Oh, well, that's wonderful!" the salesgirl told him. She rang up his merchandise. "That'll be eighty-seven dollars and fifty-three cents."

Jerrell peeled off ninety dollars in cash and handed it to her. "Keep the change."

"Oh, sir," she said nervously. "I can't."

Jerrell spied a container on the counter asking for charitable donations. "Then, give it to Jerry's Kids." Jerrell turned and walked out of the store with his merchandise.

Gena pulled up to the motel and spied Rasun standing just outside one of the rooms. She parked, climbed out of her vehicle, and made her way over to him. Rasun wrapped his arms around her and hugged her tightly, as if he were a true-blue friend.

"It's so good to see you," Gena told him.

"You're looking good," Rasun replied.

"You are too," Gena told him.

Rasun shook his head. "Not me. I'm going bald so fast, I'll look like a bowling ball in a few more weeks."

Gena laughed.

"Come on in, let's talk," Rasun told her. He turned and walked into the motel room as Gena followed close behind.

"So, what's going on, Rasun?" Gena asked. She seated herself in one of the motel room's accent chairs.

Rasun seated himself on the bed. "How are you doing, Gena?"

Gena nodded. "I'm good. I'm really good."

"Do you think about him a lot?" Rasun asked.

The question made Gena frown. She found it peculiar. "I do. We're talking about Quadir, right?"

Rasun nodded. "I think about my nigga a lot. I miss him."

"I do too," Gena said softly. "Rasun, what's the matter?"

Rasun shook his head, allowing a tear to roll down his cheek. "I'm in trouble, Gena, a whole lot of trouble."

"What is it?" Gena asked, full of concern, leaning forward in her seat.

"This bust was a bad one, Gena," he explained. "They got a lot of stuff on us. It looks real bad."

Gena shook her head sadly. "Rasun, I'm so sorry."

"I got this lawyer, but he's full of shit!" Rasun explained. "He ain't doing shit to help me. I went to some other lawyers and I showed the paperwork that I have, the indictment and everything, and they all want an arm and a leg to defend me. I don't have that kind of bread, Gena. I don't . . ."

"Have you talked to Rik?" Gena asked.

"Rik don't got it like that either," Rasun told her. "They seized everything."

Gena nodded.

"Gena, I don't want to get in your business like that or nothing, but I know that my man Qua was papered up. I know he left you papered up. You think that you could spot a brother until I worked this shit out and got back up on my feet?"

Gena recoiled. She hadn't been expecting this, and instead

of saying "I don't got it, I can't help you" she said the entirely wrong thing. "How much are you talking, Rasun?"

"The lawyers are all asking for about two hundred and fifty to three hundred grand to fight this thing," he told her. "It's a pretty big fucking conspiracy case."

Gena shook her head. "Damn, that's a lot of dough, man. I mean, what happens if you pay them, and they can't beat the case? What happens if you go to prison?"

"I'll have to pay you when I get out," Rasun told her.

"When you get out?" Gena sat back in her seat. "Damn, baby! You lose this case, you getting a Star Wars date! You looking at getting out sometime in the next century. A fucking 2032 out date or some shit."

Rasun laughed. His laughter made Gena laugh. The truth was so fucked up that they couldn't do anything but laugh.

"Gena, I hated to have to come to you like this, but you the only one I know that can stand to shoot me that kinda paper," Rasun told her. "That nigga Qua had millions put away. I mean millions."

Gena's face remained passive.

Rasun sat up and leaned in toward her. "Gena, you did get Quadir's shit, didn't you? Mrs. Richards didn't fuck you out of it, did she?"

Damn, this nigga comin' at me hard. What the fuck he worried about what Qua left me or even what his mother got, for that matter? Something here smells very fishy, Gena thought to herself. She suddenly wished she hadn't come to meet Rasun. *I don't want to help him either.*

"I don't want to talk about Quadir right now," Gena told him.

"No, I was just wondering if you were all right," Rasun

told her. "I just wanted to know if you were able to help a brother out. I really need it for these lawyers, Gena. I don't want to go to jail, you know."

Gena stood. "Let me think about this, Rasun. I don't really have that kind of paper, but I might be able to help with something."

"That would be great, Gena, really," Rasun told her. He rose and followed her to the door.

"I'll call you tomorrow, okay?" Gena told him.

Rasun nodded. Gena leaned forward and kissed him on his cheek before turning and walking away.

The door leading to the adjoining suite opened as Rasun was closing the motel room door.

"You almost had her," Detective Ellington told him. "You did a good job."

"Does that mean that I'm finished?" Rasun asked.

"Almost," Detective Ellington told him. "We just need for you to meet with her tomorrow and see what she says about the money. We just need her to admit to having the money."

"And if I get her to admit it, then I'm finished?" Rasun asked. "Am I free once I do this?"

"Rasun, you'll be free," Detective Ellington told him. "Free to keep your ass where we can find you when we need you. Until all of your little friends are sleeping in federal prisons, you are on a short leash. Is that understood?"

Rasun unbuttoned his shirt and unhooked the tape recorder that he had strapped to his waist. He handed the mini-recorder to her.

Detective Ellington waved her hand. "You keep it. You'll need it for tomorrow."

Rasun turned and stormed out of the hotel room, slamming the door behind him. Detective Ellington turned and headed back into the adjoining suite to collect her gear.

Huffing and cursing under his breath, Rasun made his way across the motel parking lot. He didn't notice the black BMW pulling up alongside him.

The black-tinted window of the BMW slid down slowly, and Rasun peered into the vehicle. He jumped, and his heart stopped.

"Give me the fucking tape," the driver told him.

"What the fuck!" Rasun exclaimed. "How?"

"Shut the fuck up and give me the tape," the driver told him.

Rasun immediately tossed the recorder to the driver.

"You fucking snitch. I can't fucking believe you, nigga," the driver sneered. He lifted his weapon and fired ten shots into Rasun before peeling off into the night.

Detectives Ellington and Davis heard the shots from their motel room. They ran out into the parking lot with their weapons drawn.

"Over here!" Dickie Davis shouted.

He raced to where Rasun was lying on the ground shaking. Letoya raced to her confidential informant and dropped to her knees beside him.

"What happened?" she shouted.

"Who did this?" Dickie Davis asked. He lifted Rasun's head off the ground.

Rasun began convulsing violently.

"We're losing him!" Dickie shouted. He lifted his walkie-talkie. "I need an EMS unit at the motel on Chestnut!" He shouted the address. "I repeat, officer requesting a medical unit to the motel on Chestnut! Gunshot victim going into shock!"

Dickie Davis laid Rasun's head down, ripped open his shirt, and began beating on Rasun's chest. Detective Ellington began breathing into Rasun's mouth.

"One, two, three, four!" Detective Davis counted as he pumped Rasun's chest.

Detective Ellington desperately tried to breathe into Rasun's mouth.

Rasun's eyes rolled back, and his body went limp. They could hear the sirens of the EMS unit growing closer with each second. Time was of the essence, and they knew that they were losing him.

THE M IS DEAD

Mark crept through the front door of Skip's dark apartment, peering around the eerie living room. Everything inside told him to leave immediately, and that nothing good would come from this trip, but still, he had to see why he had been summoned to this place. Mark pulled out his pistol, pulled back the slide, and chambered a round. He was going to shoot at the first shadow that he saw moving.

Mark's eyes slowly began adapting to the darkness of the apartment, and he began to be able to make out shapes. One of the first shapes that he was able to make out was that of a lamp. He walked to the end table and leaned forward to turn the lamp on. He froze when he felt the pressure of cold steel placed behind his ear.

"Don't move, and don't try anything stupid," Jerrell told him. "Put the gun down."

Mark opened his hand, allowing the gun to fall to the ground.

"Good," Jerrell said quietly. "Now turn on the lamp."

Mark twisted the knob, turning on the lamp and brightening the room, bringing clarity to all of the objects inside.

"What's going on, Jerrell?" Mark asked. "Where's Skip?"

Jerrell shoved Mark down onto the couch. "I'm asking the questions, nigga, not you!"

Mark's head struck the back of the couch, causing him to check his forehead for blood. He turned toward Jerrell and sat up on the couch.

"What the fuck's going on, J?" Mark asked.

"Collection time," Jerrell told him. "Where the fuck's my money?"

"Your money?" Mark looked off and smacked his lips. "Man, is that all you can think about? Somebody is out here killing off our brothers, and you're worried about your money!"

Jerrell looked at Mark like he was stupid. He couldn't believe that his dumb ass still hadn't figured shit out.

"This was supposed to be a Junior Mafia meeting," Mark shouted. "Where's everybody else?"

Jerrell smiled and lifted his arms into the air. "This is everybody! We're it, just me and you, baby!"

Mark frowned. He didn't find Jerrell's humor funny.

"I hereby call this meeting to order," Jerrell told him. "Well, I guess the first order of business is to read the minutes from the last meeting. Any volunteers? You, sir, over there on the couch, how about you?"

Mark sat on the couch sour-faced.

"Okay, well, I move that we skip the reading of the minutes and get down to business," Jerrell continued. "Today's meeting is about money. It's time to pay your dues!"

"Where's Skip?" Mark asked.

Jerrell peered down at the floor. Mark's eyes followed Jerrell's down to the floor, where he noticed for the first time that there was tape on the carpet. Mark's eyes followed the circuit of the tape, and he quickly came to realize that the tape was actually a chalk outline for a body. He jumped.

"Whoa!" Jerrell told him. He pointed his weapon at Mark. "Have a seat, nigga, and hold your horses."

Mark sat back down on the couch. "What the fuck's going on?"

"You asked where Skip was," Jerrell told him. "Just answering your question."

Mark shook his head. "You killed him?"

"Where's my money?" Jerrell asked.

Mark shook his head. "Man, I don't have any money! I have to get the fuck outta town with the quickness, remember? I've been on the run, I didn't have no time to hustle!"

"Oh, so you still have all of the dope that I fronted you then?" Jerrell asked.

Mark shifted his gaze to the ground.

"That's what I thought," Jerrell told him. "You had time to hustle my dope, but no time to put my money away."

"I needed some ends to get out of town, and to lay low," Mark tried to explain. "That's what I used the money for. Hell, it wasn't like I fucked it off! I can hustle and make it back."

Jerrell pulled out a pair of handcuffs and tossed them to Mark. "Put these on."

Mark caught the cuffs and peered up at Jerrell. "Why should I? If you gonna kill me, then do it here."

"I ain't gonna kill you, nigga," Jerrell told him. "Not unless you make me. Now put the damn cuffs on!"

Mark placed the cuffs over his wrists and snapped them closed, handcuffing himself in the front. Jerrell walked to the couch and pulled him up off it. He shoved Mark across the living-room floor and out of the front door of the apartment. Mark headed for the cars parked out front, but Jerrell tugged him away from the cars and shoved him straight ahead. He soon found himself heading toward what appeared to be a train yard, not Amtrak and not Septa, but definitely train tracks that ran through town.

"Right here," Jerrell told him.

Mark felt Jerrell place a cuff around his ankle and lock it. He peered down in time to see Jerrell lock the other side of the cuff to the railroad track. He watched as Jerrell repeated the procedure with his other leg. He was now shackled to the railroad tracks.

Jerrell lifted his pistol, turned it around, and struck Mark with the grip of his handgun. Mark fell to the ground as blood poured from his head. Jerrell knelt and handcuffed his right hand to one side of the track.

"What the fuck are you doing?" Mark asked. His head was spinning, and he was dazed. He could feel Jerrell cuffing his other hand to the other side of the railroad track. He didn't realize the full implications of Jerrell's actions until he felt a slight vibration in the tracks. The vibrations were growing stronger.

"Okay, Jerrell," Mark told him. "I get your point. I'll give you all of the money that I have left. It's almost enough to pay you back. It's like forty-five thousand dollars. You can have it, it's yours."

Jerrell stood over Mark and shook his head. "Now you

want to pay me back. It took me handcuffing you to a rail-road track to pay me back."

Mark tugged at the handcuffs, trying to free himself. "Look, I'll pay you back! You can have the money, and I'll get the rest of it to you within a week. Now please uncuff me."

The light from a freight train could be seen in the distance.

"Man, come on, this shit ain't funny no more!" Mark told him. "Come on, I'll take you to get your fucking money!"

Jerrell stepped off the track, peered down at Mark, and smiled.

Mark felt the vibrations of the train nearing; they were getting stronger and stronger as each second passed.

"I'll give you all of your shit tonight! I'll get the rest of that shit from my pops! I'll give you everything that I owe you, tonight! Uncuff me!"

Mark pulled at the cuffs desperately.

"Jerrell! This is some bullshit! We're brothers, nigga! We're Junior Mafia for life!"

"If we're Junior Mafia for life, then you got about thirty seconds before you're not Junior Mafia anymore," Jerrell told him. He turned and began to walk away.

"Jerrell! Jerrell! You can't do this, homie!" Mark shouted. He could hear the train's horn blaring nonstop and feel the tracks vibrating violently. "Jerrell! I'll give you more than what I owe you! I'll give you a hundred grand! A hundred thousand dollars tonight!"

The freight train was loaded to the hilt with grain. It felt like a strong gust of wind blowing by him when it ran over Mark. Jerrell heard the brief scream, a squashing sound, and then nothing else; there was nothing else. Mark had disappeared from the face of the earth. He was now bits and pieces of blood and tissue beneath a freight train.

"Have a safe trip," joked Jerrell as he walked back to his car.

Gena opened the door to Gah Git's house and crept inside. It was real early in the morning and the whole house was still sleeping. Gena crept up the steps and slowly down the hall to Gah Git's door. She peeked inside to see her grandmother sleeping. Quietly she tiptoed over to the side of Gah Git's bed and leaned down. She stroked her grandmother's forehead and Gah Git's eyes widened.

"Where you been?" Gah Git asked.

"Nowhere, just needed some time, that's all," Gena said, still stroking her grandmother's forehead.

"You couldn't call me and let me know you was all right? I got to get bits and pieces from everybody else," said Gah Git, as she grabbed Gena's hand and looked at her. "You all right?"

"Mmm hmm, I'm okay. It's all okay. I'm not mad anymore, and I'm sorry I didn't call you," said Gena, hugging her grandmother. Gah Git returned the embrace, happy to see Gena safe and sound.

"You know, life always has a way of dishin' out what's least expected at the most least expecting time. I think the test is really in how gracious we can respond to it all, and I think you handled the situation like an adult woman, and I'm so proud of you."

"I really don't know how to handle it all though. I mean, what am I suppose to do?"

"Just take one day at a time. That's all, just take one day at a time," Gah Git said, patting her on the back. "Just take one day at a time."

Captain Holiday chucked the thick manila folder at the gathered detectives, striking the wall just beside Letoya Ellington's head. Loose papers flew everywhere.

"What in the fuck were you thinking!" Captain Holiday shouted. "Oh, change that! You weren't thinking! You couldn't have been thinking! You don't have a fucking brain to think! Not pulling the kinda shit you just pulled!"

"Captain, I'm sorry," Letoya told him.

"Sorry!" the captain shouted. "You're sorry? A man is dead because of you! I just left a meeting with the chief and the goddamned city councilman, and both of them chewed my ass out! Do you know the kind of shitstorm you've got this department facing?"

"Sir—" Dickie Davis tried to intervene.

"Shut the fuck up!" the captain bellowed. He looked as though he were about to pop a blood vessel in his forehead. "I didn't ask you to fucking speak. Detective Davis, when I want your goddamned opinion, I'll let you know!"

Captain Holiday turned and lit up a fat Cuban cigar. He scowled at Detective Davis with disdain. "Fucking numb nuts!"

"Sir, we had the situation controlled," Ratzinger told him. "The CI was killed while he was leaving the scene. He was no longer under Detective Ellington's control."

"Bullshit!" Captain Holliday shouted. "That CI is under your control until you safely tuck his ass into bed at night! You know that, I know that, everybody knows that! If the media gets ahold of this shit, it's our ass! Do you hear me, it's our ass! And the mayor has already made it clear that if this thing blows up, heads will roll! Somebody is going to have to fall on their goddamned sword, and it sure as hell ain't gonna be me! You got that, Lieutenant? Badges! I'm collecting fucking badges, gold ones, green ones, and silver ones included!"

"Sir—"

"Shit rolls downhill, Sergeant!" Captain Holiday shouted at Letoya Ellington. "Now does someone want to tell me what the fuck you had a CI doing out at that time of the night, on an operation that was not sanctioned by me? Seeing as how you all work for me, I'd like to know about the little operations that you have going on, don't you think?"

Letoya nodded. "Yes, sir!"

"Well, let's hear it, Detective," the captain told her. "What the fuck was going on?"

"Sir, Detective Davis and I, during the course of questioning the confidential informant, learned that there may actually be another large drug ring operating in the city," she explained. "Perhaps as large as the one we just took down."

Captain Holiday leaned back in his overstuffed leather chair. "And just how did you come to this conclusion?"

"The girlfriend of one Quadir Richards, who was actually the previous leader of the group that we took down, has a new boyfriend who is providing her with quite a lavish lifestyle," Ellington explained. "It's this boyfriend who we believe is part of the other drug ring. We wanted to target him, and then branch out and track all of the members of his organization, and even roll up his supply chain."

"And his name, Sergeant?" Captain Holiday asked.

"We were trying to ascertain that information on the night the CI was killed, sir," she explained. "He was meeting with

Gena Scott, Quadir Richards's former love interest, to ascertain the name of her new boyfriend."

"And then he was killed?" the captain asked. "Any idea who did this?"

Dickie Davis shook his head. "None, sir."

"Why in the hell did you two try to play Starsky and Hutch, and go at it alone?" the captain asked angrily. "Why didn't you go through the proper channels, and set up a proper operation, so that you could have enough officers to back you up? What, do you two think that you're Don Johnson and Phillip Michael Thomas now?"

"We were under time constraints, sir," Detective Ellington told him.

"Bullshit!" Captain Holiday told them. "This had the makings of a long-term operation. You just told me you wanted to roll up the entire organization, Sergeant!"

"Yes, but the window for meeting with the girlfriend and obtaining this information was narrowing, sir," Davis added. "We used the CI's arrest as an excuse for the meeting. He was asking her for money, and talking to her about moving on after the death of her husband, and trying to gain her sympathy and trust, sir."

Captain Holiday shook his head. "I'm too old a cat to be fooled by a bunch of kittens; this thing stinks. The whole damn thing stinks to high heaven. Let me tell you all something, and listen up real good. I've got a pissed-off mayor, a super-hot city councilman, and a furious chief chewing on my ass. I've got Internal Affairs looking into this whole incident. One thing looks suspect, and I'm collecting your badges, and having all of your asses thrown in jail. Is that clear?"

Detective Ratzinger, Detective Davis, and Sergeant Ellington all nodded.

"If the press gets wind that this was a police operation, and that this guy was killed while working undercover for the department, your careers are effectively over," Captain Holiday told them. "And I'm going to hand them your asses. And they are going to crucify you. Or what's left of you, because the department is going to run for cover, and let them know that this was an unauthorized operation."

Captain Holiday leaned back in his chair and examined the three officers standing before him. Something was fishy. He couldn't put his finger on it, but the whole damn affair stank. He blew a giant circle of cigar smoke into the air toward them and frowned.

"Get the hell out of my office," Holiday told them.

THE VERDICT'S OUT

Jerrell wrapped his arms around Gena and pulled her close. She rested her head against his shoulders and closed her eyes. The wind blowing on her face felt good to her. It felt relaxing, purifying almost. She was happier than she had been in a long time. She had her a good man, a new apartment, two cars, plenty of money, and a baby on the way. Life couldn't have been better for her.

Jerrell turned her face toward his and kissed her deeply, passionately. She felt his kiss work its way from her lips through her body, and all the way down to her toes. She became lost in it.

The park was empty today, with one or two others milling about. Most of the usual parkgoers were at work at this time. So they pretty much had the park and all its greenery to themselves. It was the benefit of not having a regular nine to five. They were free to do as they pleased, whenever they pleased.

"Want some more cake?" Gena asked.

Jerrell waved his hand, turning down her offer. "No thanks, baby. I'm pretty full."

"What?" Gena asked with a smile. "You didn't like my cake? I made it just for you."

"No, I loved it," Jerrell told her. "I loved the whole meal, baby. I ate like a pig, don't you think?"

Gena's eyes narrowed. "Uh-hun."

"What? Are you trying to get me fat or something?" Jerrell asked playfully. "What are you going to do when I try to climb on top of you all fat and greasy and stuff? Are you still going to give me some loving?"

Jerrell tickled her side, and Gena tried to knock his hands away.

"Are you still going to let me work that thang?" he asked, while still tickling her.

"Maybe," Gena said, laughing and fighting his hands away.

Gena grabbed a slice of cake and smeared it onto Jerrell's lips. She leaped up from the picnic blanket on which they were lying and took off into the park. Jerrell leaped to his feet and chased her.

Gena cut through the playground area and stopped just on the other side of a large, colorful slide. Jerrell chased after her, and she quickly raced to the other side of the slide.

"You aren't going to catch me," Gena told him.

"That's only because you got me full," Jerrell told her, while breathing heavily. "I have another idea."

"And what's that?" she asked.

Jerrell turned and raced back toward their picnic basket. On the way he turned and shouted in her direction. "I'm going to drink up all of the Moët!"

Gena took off running toward the picnic basket. She arrived just after he did and dove on top of him. Jerrell dropped the bottle and grabbed her. Together they rolled around on the blanket until he found himself on top of her, staring into her eyes. Slowly, he leaned forward and kissed her passionately.

It was as if they were kissing for the first time, Gena felt. She had become turned out on him more than anything else. His sex was good, real good, and like a magnet. She kept wanting more and more of him, all of him that she could get. And it wasn't just the sex that she was falling for; he was a protector. He had vowed to protect her and kept telling her he would keep her safe and he'd never let anyone cause her any harm. She loved hearing how she'd be protected, and more than just being lost in his arms, she found herself lost in him. She couldn't believe that she could feel this way again, but in a way, she had a deep, caring love for Jerrell. It wasn't driven by passion, but it was driven by a yearning to just be loved.

She could definitely see herself spending the rest of her life with this man. She could definitely see herself waking up in his arms, cooking his meals, and having his children. For the first time in a long time, she could honestly say that she was genuinely happy.

United States District Attorney Paul Perachetti strolled into the room wearing one of his usual three-thousand-dollar Armani suits. He looked the part of a district attorney. He was tanned and toned, with graying sideburns and an always fresh haircut. He looked more like an expensive Mafia lawyer than a district attorney. His Rolex watches, dark Italian suits, and the Cadillac Seville that he drove certainly made it seem as though he were mob-affiliated, not to mention the fact that he was Sicilian through and through.

The gathered officers, detectives, and agents all spoke in hushed whispers, wondering why they had been summoned to the federal building today. Many guessed that it was another major operation that the Feds wanted them to take part in. The fact that there were several assistant United States district attorneys whispering in the ear of the district attorney made them all nervous. And the fact that there was a United States district judge and a United States magistrate in on the whispering made the entire affair seem even more ominous. Even the FBI agents were nervous.

"What do you think it is?" Detective Davis asked his partner.

Letoya shook her head. "I don't know. Whatever it is, it can't be good."

"All these damn Feds in one room makes me nervous," Dickie said.

"We're all law enforcement officers," Detective Ellington told him. "Besides, the Feds look like they are nervous too."

There were about fifteen United States marshals inside the room already when another fifteen to twenty walked into the room and stood at the rear, as if they were guarding the door.

"What the fuck's going on in here, Sergeant?" DEA agent Stacey Wynn asked Letoya.

She shook her head. "Hell, you're a Fed, you should know more about this than I do."

Up front, the district attorney finished speaking with one of the deputy district attorneys, the federal district court judge, and the federal district court magistrate. There were lots of whispers and nods exchanged. The district attorney turned toward the room full of law enforcement officers and cleared his throat. Instantly, the room grew deathly silent.

"Gentlemen, and ladies, as most of you know, my name is Paul Perachetti, and I am the United States district attorney for this district. I know some of you, and some of you I've seen your face a time or two, but haven't had the pleasure of getting to know you. I asked you all to come here today so that I can look you in the eye and give you my deepest and most sincere apology, and express to each of you my personal regret."

Murmurs echoed throughout the room, as the gathered law enforcement personnel wondered what the district attorney was talking about.

"Recently, we conducted a multiagency operation in this city that resulted in numerous arrests," Paul Perachetti continued. "We seized hundreds of weapons, millions of dollars in vehicles, jewelry, and other personal property, and were able to remove hundreds of drug dealers from the street."

The gathered law enforcement agents broke into applause.

Perachetti held up his hand to silence them. "During the course of this event, we gathered numerous pieces of evidence, the primary evidence being electronic pin gathering, telephone monitoring, video surveillance, and wire recordings gathered by a confidential informant. This evidence was in the hands of a federal agency and has unfortunately been mishandled. I apologize to all of you who worked so hard and made so many sacrifices to gather this evidence. I take full responsibility for everything that has happened, as I should have shown more diligence in safeguarding this material, instead of delegating that duty. I am the United States district attorney, and the buck stops here. So I want to personally apologize to all of you."

Agent Wynn raised his hand.

Paul Perachetti pointed toward him. "Yes, Agent Wynn?"

"What are you saying?" Agent Wynn asked. "Are you saying that all of the electronic surveillance evidence is missing? Is it lost, misplaced, or what?"

Paul Perachetti cleared his throat. "What I am saying is that the evidence was mishandled, and that all of the recordings have been destroyed."

"Destroyed?" another agent asked.

"I'm sorry, I don't know all of you, and I regret that fact," Perachetti told them. "So, I would ask everyone to state their names and the agency they work for, when they ask a question. That way I know who I'm talking to, and I can get to learn your name, and be able to put a face with your name in the future."

"Matthew Sauls, FBI," the agent stated. "So, when you say destroyed, do you mean literally destroyed, like it's been smashed or something?"

"Good question," Perachetti told him. "When I say destroyed, I mean that the evidence is no longer usable. The disks have been somehow magnetically wiped clean."

Letoya lifted her hand.

"Yes?" Perachetti asked, pointing to her.

"Sergeant Letoya Ellington, Philadelphia Narcotics Division," she told him. "Wiped clean? All of them? And how did this happen?"

"The disks were stored in a metal cool storage unit, and on the other side of the room, Federal Security Police were using a large X-ray-screening device for security purposes," Perachetti explained. "Apparently, the device emitted some sort of magnetic current that found its way into the metal storage container in the next room and cleared all of the disks. That's all I know."

Another agent raised his hand.

"Yes?" Perachetti asked, calling on the gentleman.

"Anthony Hopkins, Alcohol, Tobacco, and Firearms. Sir, how the hell did this happen?"

The United States marshals in the rear of the room stirred uneasily. That was when Sergeant Ellington realized why they were there. They were there for the protection of the district attorney.

"No one ever thought that the placement of this new cool storage locker would be affected by the magnetic radiation being emitted by the scanning device on the other side of the wall," Perachetti explained. "This is a new storage device, just purchased and installed by DEA, and this had never happened before. It was just one of those things that no one could have foreseen."

"Sir, what does all of this mean?"

"I'm sorry," Perachetti told him. "Your name and agency, please?"

"Oh, sorry," the agent said sheepishly. "Cody Coil, DEA. Sir, what does all of this mean in layman's terms?"

"It means that we have lost all of our evidence," Perachetti said matter-of-factly.

"Agent Nick Best, FBI, sir. Have we tried some deep data recovery on the disks, sir?"

Perachetti nodded. "The disks were sent over to NSA, so that their technicians could work some of their magic on them. NSA couldn't get it done. They recommended the

Navy's cryptologist, so we sent the disks over to the Navy. They couldn't recover any data, so we sent them over to NASA, and still no luck. We have pretty much exhausted all resources. We even had a guy over at CIA write a special recovery program, and that fell through. The data is irrecoverable."

"Joseph Cannon, FBI, sir. So what does all of this mean?"

"I'm glad you asked that question, Agent Cannon," Perachetti told him. "The bottom line is, we have no evidence to try the accused with."

Murmurs shot through the room.

"Sir, Nick Best again. Are you saying that they are going to walk?"

Agent Cannon raised his hand.

Perachetti called on him.

"Sir, we still have the confidential informant," Agent Cannon said. "His testimony before the jury, as well as any new evidence that he could gather from new communications intercepts . . ."

Perachetti looked down and shook his head. "Gentlemen, I regret to inform you that the confidential informant that was utilized to gather most of the evidence in this case was killed a few nights ago, in what appeared to be a random homicide."

"This is bullshit!" Agent Anthony Hopkins shouted. "We busted our asses, risked our lives, and now you are telling us that these scumbags are going to walk!"

"Gentlemen, you all have my sincerest apologies," Perachetti told them. "I know the amount of energy, the amount of sacrifice, and the dedication that you all put in to the case. I want to assure you that my office will do all that it can to salvage this case. I just wanted to let you know where we stood, and to apologize to you personally."

"Fucking DEA!" several agents shouted anonymously.

"Hey, fuck you!" a DEA agent shouted.

"Gentlemen, please!" the judge shouted. He had heard enough. He had an evidence hearing coming up, and he knew that many of the defendants' attorneys would be pressing him to proceed, and pressuring the district attorney's office to share the evidence that they had against their clients. Pages and pages of blank transcripts would not do the trick. He faced the unpleasant prospect of having to rule in the defendants' favor, based on the lack of evidence. He would have to kick all of them back out onto the streets.

A dead confidential informant, the judge thought. *How convenient. How fucking convenient.* He wondered if the officers and attorneys working this case could screw things up any worse than they already had. *Cluster fuck* was the term that entered into his mind.

YOU LOSE TO WIN

Gena was seated on the floor of her new apartment, pulling out the home décor accessories that she had purchased from Neiman Marcus, Crate and Barrel, and Fortunoff's. Packaging paper that had been used to wrap the various porcelain, crystal, and ceramic items was scattered throughout her living room. She couldn't believe that she was finally at this point in her life.

Markita stepped over several of the valuable items as she made her way into Gena's kitchen for another glass of soda. Tracey was seated at the glass breakfast table unwrapping more of Gena's little odds and ends and wiping them clean with a slightly damp cloth.

"Girl, you want something to drink?" Markita asked, holding up a bottle of Sprite.

"My doctor said sodas are the worst. Dr. Amerson said to only drink water," Gena told her.

"What about juice?" asked Tracey.

"Only in the morning with breakfast. She said she'd rather

me eat fruit instead of drinking juice because of all the sugar."

"Oh, Lord, here we go and you ain't even out the first trimester yet. I can see this gonna be a long nine months. I'll just be glad when my little godbaby gets here," Markita told her.

"Our little goddaughter!" Tracey corrected her.

"What makes you so sure that it's going to be a girl?" Gena asked.

"How did he have your legs up when you got pregnant? That will tell you right there," Markita said in all seriousness.

Gena and Tracey broke into laughter.

"What the fuck are you talking about now?" Gena asked.

"Girl, if the nigga had ya legs straight up in the air and he was digging up in that shit deeper than a muthafucka, then it's a girl," Markita explained. "If you was riding him or if he had you doggie style when he nutted, then, it's a boy."

"How in the fuck do you figure that?" Tracey shouted. She and Gena were laughing their asses off.

"Kita, where do you get this shit from?" Gena asked.

Markita nodded. "All right, just watch, you'll see. Y'all ho's think that Markita don't know what the fuck I'm talking about, but I do, and when I try to tell you something you don't wanna listen."

"Whatever," joked Tracey.

"Look, Gena, do you want some juice or what?"

"Yeah, dag!" Gena told her.

Markita grabbed a glass from the counter and poured Gena some orange juice. She placed the OJ container back inside the refrigerator and then turned toward Tracey. "Do you want something to drink while I'm over here?"

Still laughing, Tracey shook her head. "No, I'm good."

"Y'all ho's gonna learn to pay attention when I'm trying to tell y'all something," she told them both, pointing her finger at them, while taking the glass of orange juice to Gena.

Gena and Tracey continued laughing. Finally, Gena held her arms out toward Markita.

"Awwww, my baby is mad," Gena said in a pouting tone. "Come and give sister a hug. Come on over here, Tracey. We gonna give Kita a group hug."

Tracey rose from the table and joined Gena on the floor. She opened her arms toward a pouting Markita.

"Fuck y'all, you know that?" Markita told them, as she walked to where they were and fell into their arms. "I hate y'all bitches."

Gena, Markita, and Tracey hugged, and then broke into laughter. Markita rubbed Gena's stomach.

"So, what did Jay say when you told him about the baby?" she asked.

Gena shook her head. "I haven't told him yet."

"What?" Tracey shouted. "Why haven't you told him?"

"I'm waiting for the right moment," Gena said.

"The right moment?" Markita repeated. "Bitch, when is that, during delivery?"

Tracey and Markita laughed.

"Are you afraid to tell him, or something?" Tracey asked.

Gena shook her head. "Of course not. Girl, it's just that once I actually tell him, the shit will become real."

"Girl, the shit is already real!" Tracey told her. "What are you talking about?"

Gena shrugged. "I don't know. It just seems like it would

become a lot more real, once I tell him. I don't know. I guess I figure that once I tell him, all of the bullshit would start."

"Is he a sorry-ass nigga?" Tracey asked.

Gena shook her head.

"Is he a deadbeat muthafucka?" Markita asked.

"No, he's not like that at all," Gena told them.

"Then, girl, why are you tripping?" Tracey asked. "You say he's not like that."

"I know, but I don't want him to become like that," Gena told them. "Babies have a way of complicating things. Besides, we've never talked about babies, or family, or any of those things."

"Gena, what are you thinking?" Tracey asked. "Are you thinking that you can just go nine months without telling him, and then pop up with a baby one day?"

"Your stomach is gon' get big, you do know that?" Markita told her.

Gena nodded and pulled her legs close. She wrapped her arms around her legs and rested her chin on her knees. "I just don't want things to change between us."

"Girl, you're going to have a baby," Markita told her. "Sorry to burst your bubble, but everything's gonna change."

Gena nodded and peered off into space. *They're right, my life is going to change.*

The heavy steel door slowly opened and Rik walked through it with his big bundle of paperwork. He had motion after motion and brief after brief tucked beneath his arm. His attorney had definitely been busy. He had to remember that for future reference. It was rare to find a drug attorney who actually did some work for his clients. He would definitely use this guy again, if it ever came to it.

Rik waited at the elevator door for the guard to arrive and take him downstairs to process out to freedom. He had prayed every single night to be delivered from the clutches of the powers that be, and someone upstairs had definitely heard his prayers.

His lawyer said that the case had been dismissed for lack of evidence. How that could be was beyond him. When they were first arrested, the lawyers said that the DEA had tapes on top of tapes of recorded conversations from phone taps, wired informants, and pager intercepts. They had enough shit on him to make the transcriptions of his recordings thicker than a New York phone book. And now, apparently, it was all gone.

Poof. Rik smiled, as he stepped onto the elevator. Just like that; from a mountain of evidence, to none at all. He wasn't quite sure what had happened, and neither was his attorney, but apparently there had been a problem with the tapes. *Beautiful! Fucking beautiful.* He really didn't care what had happened to those tapes, just so long as something had happened to them. He wasn't down for spending the rest of his life in some underground fucking federal prison in Colorado, or some fucking U.S. pen in bubble-fuck-god-knows-where with the KKK pretending to be a fucking correctional officer.

"What the fuck are you smiling about, asshole?" the deputy working the elevator asked him.

"America," Rik told him. "America the land of the free. I love this country!"

The guard frowned. He knew about the big kickout, and

like all of the other pigs, he wasn't exactly happy about it. They would have to give back all of the shit that had been seized as well. He probably had his fucking eye on one of his partners' Rolexes or something, and was mad 'cause he couldn't steal it at police auction for a hundred bucks now. Fuck him. He chose his profession, like everyone else chose theirs. If he wanted to wear chuck jewelry and roll in a Range, a Benz, or a BMW, then he should have chosen a different profession. He was a hater, like all of the rest. Mad because he had to get up early in the morning, put on a tight uniform, and fight traffic. *They couldn't pay me enough to watch dicks all fucking day,* Rik thought. And that brought him to his second line of thought.

In order to get his shit back, he would have to prove that he had had the income to purchase it. He would have to show receipts, tax returns, check stubs, and all of that other bullshit. He had none of those things. And he damn sure couldn't claim the millions of dollars that those fucking pigs seized from his stash house, which meant that all of his hard-earned savings were wiped out. The DEA would certainly be on their asses again, waiting for them to so much as jaywalk. He wouldn't be able to spit on a sidewalk without the Feds swooping down on him, especially in Philly. He had to take his show on the road and find a new city to live in. And he had to do it quietly, so that the Feds wouldn't know where he relocated to.

The problem with finding a new spot for Rik was that he was worried about not knowing the town, the players, or how the niggas got down. Not to mention the way guys were snitching on each other these days; it wasn't good. But Rik needed bread, like yesterday. He had overhead, not to mention he needed some new wheels and another crib. He needed to come up and he needed to come up fast. He needed a jack move; he needed to play stickup kid one last time, to get some score fair. The problem with that was that most of the niggas that he knew had got caught up in the bust and everybody was sort of in the same predicament he was, waiting for the next couple months to get back the shit that had been seized. Hell, they were probably all thinking the same thing that he was thinking at this very moment. *Who the fuck can I rob out here to hold me over until I get my shit back from the government, if I ever do?*

Rik laughed at the thought of that. A bunch of broke-ass ballers, sticking each other up for peanuts. I rob this nigga one night, and another nigga comes through the window and gets me the following night. Naw, he needed to get away from them fools, and to catch a come up that nobody else knew about. He needed a mark that he could keep to himself, and hit all by himself. Only one target like that came to mind.

Clair opened her door to find a box sitting on her front porch. She peered around, wondering who had rung her doorbell at this time of the night, but could see only the red taillights of a big black sedan driving away. It looked like a BMW or a Mercedes, or some other type of expensive car. *Why is people ringing my bell and then just driving off like that? Crazy asses,* she thought. But then, this had been a crazy week for her. It was as if the entire world had gone mad.

The only reason that she had even opened up her door was that she thought it was probably some old friends of her son's, wanting to pay their respects. Rasun had had many friends, and many of them had come by already. More and more were showing up with each passing day, now that their cases had been dropped and they were filtering out of the jails. But none of them could offer her the help that she so desperately needed, because they were all dealing with their own issues at this time. It was something that she understood.

She didn't have any insurance on Rasun. She hadn't had any since he was a small child. She and her husband hadn't been able to afford it. Times had been tough while he was growing up, and even tougher in recent years. She knew that he was out there hustling, and she knew the consequences that that lifestyle held, but life insurance was something that she simply could not afford, not unless she wanted to skip something called eating. So she found herself in her present dilemma, not having enough money to bury her child.

She set the large black box on top of her kitchen table and pulled the ribbon off it, so that she could open it. Once this was done, she carefully lifted the large lid and peered inside. To her astonishment, she found wads of money and a note. Clair grabbed the note, placed her hand on her chest, and reseated herself. In a shocked, monotonous clip, she read the note aloud.

"Dear Clair: Please accept this money as a token of my love for your son, and as a sign of our friendship. There is enough money inside of the box to pay the cost of his burial, and to help you with all of your bills. I'll do what I can from time to time."

Clair crumpled the note in her hand and broke down into tears, happy, sad, and confused as to who would give her all this money.

ON AND POPPIN'

I love you so much!" Gena said as she opened her legs wider, allowing him full access to her most private of possessions.

"I love you too, baby," Jerrell lied. He went into her deeply, feeling her viselike clamp around him. It was torture, almost. Torture because it felt so good, and torture that he had to waste some of the best pussy that had ever been put on the planet. But for now, he was going to make the most of it.

Gena wrapped her arms around his back and kissed her man passionately. Tonight, she wanted him to have all of her. She was going to throw it back at him, and take all of the pain that she knew was coming. She wanted to fully become his, to mold herself to his body. She was going to share with him the news of the life that they had created together. She was going to share with him her plans for their future.

Jerrell kissed her passionately. He had never felt her like this before. He was inside her, working her, trying to savor her tight canal. It felt as if she were gripping at his manhood with a tight fist. She was working him nearly as much as he was working her. He swallowed hard, trying not to cry out. It felt good to him. It felt like something that he had never felt before, like a level of lovemaking that he didn't know existed.

"Oh, my god!" Gena cried out. She bit down on his shoulder. She could feel him really getting into it now. It seemed as if he had grown even bigger inside her. "Oh, Jay!"

"Gena!" Jerrell grunted. Never before had a woman made him call out her name. Whatever secret she had inside her, he wished that he could bottle it up and keep it.

"Oh, Jay!" Gena cried out even louder. "It . . . it . . . it . . ."

It had begun to hurt. Jerrell was touching her in places where no one and nothing else had ever touched before. He was reaching deep inside her, stretching her out, hammering at things that clearly were not meant to be hammered. She came once, and then immediately again. She thought about how she must feel to him, being deep inside her, gutting her, stretching out her interior walls. The thought of his pleasure made her come again. She could feel water flowing inside her as if she had turned on some secret faucet.

"Gena . . ." he cried out again. Jerrell could feel himself tightening up. He wanted to explode inside her. Never before in his life had he not been able to control his orgasms. Never before in his life had he been reduced to being a fifteen-minute man. No, he had hour power at least. He had the ability to make passionate love for hours on end, and sometimes even into the wee hours of the morning. But this, this was something completely different, something completely new to him. How could she do this to him?

Jerrell exploded inside her, shooting his fluids even deeper into her body. His deep explosion caused her to arch her back and cry out. She gasped for air and held on to him tightly. She could feel his entire body shaking. She had never felt him come like that before.

"You okay, baby?" Gena asked, rubbing his sweating back. "You're still shaking."

Embarrassed, Jerrell rolled off her and lay next to her in bed. He was tired. He had been up all the previous night, planning tonight's events. He had been on his feet all that day, wrapping up all of the loose ends, and now, he was feeling it.

Gena placed her arm beneath his head and caressed his sweating chest with her index finger. "There's something that I want to talk to you about."

"What?" he asked softly.

"It's nothing really," she told him. "It's just a little surprise that I wanted to share with you."

Jerrell yawned, closed his eyes, and quickly dozed off. Gena stared at the snoring body before her, not believing that when she finally had the courage to tell him, he fell asleep on her. She slid her arm from beneath his head and carefully slid out of the bed. She could still feel the pressure on her stomach, and it felt as though she had to use the restroom. She hoped that the room had toilet paper in it. It would be a real bitch to have to get dressed and walk all the way to the office just for some toilet paper.

Why Jay had chosen to take her to a motel room tonight puzzled her deeply. He had an apartment, and she had told him that she now had her own apartment too. They could have gone back to either of their places after dinner, so why he chose a motel so far on the outskirts of town was beyond her. The thought that he had another woman at home or nearby crossed her mind.

Gena made her way across the motel room to the bathroom. She opened the door and walked inside to find buckets, chains, and bags of cement. She also found handcuffs and rope.

"What the fuck?" she said softly. Gena closed the bathroom door and turned the lock on the knob. She didn't want to wake him, and she didn't want him walking in on her while she snooped around. She opened the shower curtain and peered in at the bathtub. There was a bucket labeled acid sitting inside it. The hairs on the back of her neck quickly stood at attention.

Gena sat down on the toilet and peed. It flowed out of her rapidly, as her pregnancy, combined with her nervousness, had worked havoc on her bladder. She quickly located a roll of toilet paper, wiped herself, and then began to snoop around some more. She found a large duffel bag beneath the bathroom counter.

Gena opened the large, green, Army-issue duffel bag and to her surprise found herself staring at millions of dollars in cash. Her mind quickly began to race. Why the bag full of money? Why the acid, the cement, the buckets, the handcuffs, the chains? He was definitely going to get rid of a body and get out of town. And being that she was the only body around, it was pretty clear what Jay had in mind. *But why?*

Gena sat back down on the toilet and began to think. *What the fuck is he doing with acid and all this money and why the fuck does he got me in this hotel room when I could be home in my own bed? This shit ain't right. I think I better get the hell outta here.* Her mind formulated questions faster than she could even begin to process them. But there was one thing that she did know for sure. She was getting the hell out of that room. Thank God she hadn't told him where her new apartment was.

Gena rose and opened the door. Jerrell was standing in the doorway.

Gena screamed and tried to close the bathroom door. Jerrell bum-rushed his way inside.

"What the fuck are you doing?" Gena screamed. "What the fuck is all this shit?"

Jerrell punched Gena in her face, grabbed her by her hair, and dragged her into the bedroom.

"You nosy bitch!" Jerrell shouted.

Gena reached up and dug her nails into Jerrell's face, scratching him deeply. "Let me go! Let me go!"

"Aaaaarrgh!" Jerrell shouted. He knocked her hands away and then slapped her with the back of his hand. Gena flew onto the bed.

"Let me out of here!" Gena leaped up off the bed and jumped at Jerrell, trying to claw his eyes out. He was going to kill her, but she wasn't going out like no crying docile bitch! This nigga was going to have to fight for his kill.

Jerrell protected his face, pushed Gena back, and then kicked her in her stomach. Gena dropped to the floor. Jerrell kicked her in her face, causing blood to shoot across the room. Gena raced to the nightstand, grabbed the lamp from it, and swung it at him. The lamp struck Jerrell on the side of his head, and blood ran down into his eye, temporarily blinding him. Gena raced for the door.

"Come here, bitch!" Jerrell shouted. He grabbed Gena just as she was opening the motel-room door.

Gena kicked and screamed. She bit down on Jerrell's forearm, causing him to drop her. Again she raced for the door.

Jerrell threw a fierce punch at her before she could open the door all of the way. The punch caught her in the back of her head, causing her to go dizzy. She fell backward, still clutching the doorknob. The door to the motel room swung open as she hit the floor. She could barely make out the shadow standing in the doorway.

"What the fuck?" Jerrell asked. "Nigga, mind your own muthafuckin' business! Don't try to be no Captain Save a Ho!"

"This is my business," he told Jerrell.

"Oh, really?" Jerrell asked. Jerrell started for the bed, where he had his gun beneath the pillow. He heard the click of another weapon.

"Go for it," the shadowy figure told him.

"Who the fuck are you?" Jerrell shouted.

The shadow stepped into the light of the motel room. Jerrell's eyes grew wider than grapefruits.

"You! This is bullshit! This can't be!" Jerrell dove for his gun. "You're supposed to be dead, nigga!"

Gunfire lit up the motel room as bullets struck Jerrell in his neck, his chest, his side, his arm, his back, and his thigh. Blood and smoke poured from his body as he lay on top of the motel-room bed.

Gena felt herself being lifted up off the floor. She felt herself in familiar arms, smelling a familiar smell. She was dizzy; her eyes had been beaten almost shut. But she was still able to barely make out the face of the man who was carrying her across the parking lot to the black BMW that had been stalking her every move. She was tired, bruised, bleeding, and growing weaker by the moment. She stared into his face and smiled. "Quadir."

Then she passed out in his arms.

DISCUSSION QUESTIONS

1. What do you think Jay's real intentions were when he offered Gena help at the gas station?

2. Do you think Gena was too trusting when Jay offered to keep her safe?

3. Was Bria's behavior due to adolescence or blatant disrespect of Gah Git?

4. Do you think Gena was careless with the way she spent Quadir's money? Would you have done anything differently?

5. Was Jay justified in killing members of the Junior Mafia, even after he found out the truth? Or do you think he was on a power trip?

6. Why do you think Champagne was so willing to help Jay, even after the way he had treated her?

7. Do you think Rasun snitched to say his family or himself?

8. If you were a police officer, would you have joined the plot to take Quadir's money? Or do you think they should have left well enough alone?

9. Do you think Gena could have done more to prevent her pregnancy? Was she genuinely happy, or do you think she was trying to make up for her loss of Quadir?

10. Are you happy that the crew got off in the end? Or do you think they should have gone down for their drug crimes?

11. Who do you think was following Gena in the BMW?

DEAR READERS

I couldn't believe it when Grand Central Publishing came to me about writing a sequel to *True to the Game*. The first thing that ran through my mind was, how? How do I write the sequel to a book that has been deemed a classic? How will I keep the spirit of my characters alive? How will I write a Part II that everyone will love just as much as they loved the first?

These were the questions that soared through my head when I thought about you, my readers. I am happy to know that you are just as thrilled to be thrown back into the lives of your favorite characters, as I have been to write about them.

I hope you enjoyed your book, and as always, thank you for your support.

Truly,

Teri Woods

AN EXCERPT FROM
TRUE TO THE GAME III

Available July 2008
wherever books are sold

Gena slowly tried to open her eyes, feeling pain beyond belief throughout her entire body. She was sore and she was bruised from her head to her toes. She looked around the room, not quite realizing where she was. Her head, left arm, rib cage, and left thigh were all bandaged. She could barely open her bruised and blackened eyes, but she managed to open them far enough to see around the room. At first she thought she was in a hospital, lying in a hospital bed. But she wasn't. The room's décor was unlike any hospital décor that she had ever seen. The more she was able to open her eyes, the more she realized she wasn't in the hospital. She was in a room, a quiet room, but she did not recognize anything. *Where am I?* She decided to make finding the answer to that question her life's mission for the moment.

With great effort, accompanied by great pain, Gena rose from the king-sized bed that she had been lying on. There was a breeze blowing through an open window, the soft silk panels billowing gently with the air. She could smell the sweet fragrance of flowers wafting through the window. *If only I could make it to the window.* She mustered up as much strength as she could, desperately wanting to know where she was.

Gena clasped one of the bed posts and made her way to the bottom of the four-post bed. From there she threw her wobbly legs forward and grabbed hold of a nearby accent chair. She braced herself using the arms of the chair, and then carefully made her way around it until she was able to grab hold of a nearby dresser. Using the dresser as a support, she slowly made her way to the open window, where she was finally able to peer outside and get a glimpse of her surroundings.

She was on the second floor of what appeared to be a home. She could see very large homes all around her. High-pitched slate, granite-tiled roofs, and well-manicured backyards with massive swimming pools and tennis courts filled her view. She peered down into the backyard just below her, and found an equally large swimming pool and adjacent tennis court, along with the fragrant garden that had attracted her attention initially. The azaleas, roses, Russian sage, gardenias, and other flora spread throughout the landscape, painted it in rich hues of blue, red, white, yellow, green, and purple. *Where the hell am I?*

Gena turned towards the dresser, and pulled open the first drawer, only to find it empty. She moved on to the second drawer, only to find it in the same state. The third, fourth, fifth, and sixth dresser drawers were also empty. She was in a guest bedroom, and there were no secrets kept here. She turned and spied two doors on the opposite side of the room. One she surmised to be a closet, while the other would have to be the guest bathroom. Hoping that the closet or the medicine cabinet would reveal something, she painfully made her way across the room towards them.

Gena opened the first door to find a row of plastic clothes hangers facing her. There was nothing on the shelves, nothing stored at the bottom of the closet, nothing period. Disappointed, she turned her attention to the next door. She had been correct in her assumptions, as the second door was to the guest bathroom. Gena braced herself on the door handle and stumbled inside. She held on to the bathroom sink and yanked open the medicine cabinet. Nothing.

"Dammit!" Gena cursed. She was growing frustrated with each passing moment. She was in a luxurious prison, all alone and wounded. She couldn't run away if she tried. Her entire body was one big ache and pain. *Think, Gena,* she told herself. *Think. What do you remember? What do you remember?*

Gena braced herself and slowly made her way back to the massive poster bed, where she lay down again. *Where am I and who brought me here?* She started to think back and remembered Jerrell. She opened the bathroom door and there it all was, the rope, *everything he had in the bathroom.* Jerrell had taken her to a motel room where he had tried to kill her. She remembered fighting him back. *Yes, I remember, but then what? What happened? Did I trip or fall or something? No, I was running for the door when he grabbed me, but what happened next?* At first Gena could not recall, then she slowly began to remember. *The gun. Someone had a gun and someone saved me.*

The question now going through Gena's mind was who had done the shooting. *Jerrell, he shot someone. He was trying to kill me and now he must have me here, holding me hostage. What the hell does he think he's doing? It doesn't even make sense. If he was going to kill me, why didn't he just go ahead and do it? No, that doesn't make sense either. He was trying to kill me. Someone else must have saved me, but who? None of this makes any sense at all.*

Nothing added up. She was bandaged but had no idea who bandaged her up. She was somewhere, but didn't have a clue as to where and she was definitely in someone's house, but again, had no idea whose. She had been in and out of consciousness, but had no idea for how long. *Someone's obviously been taking care of me,* she thought to herself. Someone had bandaged her up, given her medicine, fed her, and kept her clean. Someone had expended a lot of effort to heal her and care for her. *But who?*

Gena leaned back and closed her eyes, and her tears began to fall. Her mind had granted her an additional memory from that night, one that she knew could not be true. She had dreamed that Quadir was alive. She was barely conscious, but it all seemed so real at the time. Her Quadir had rescued her from that monster, and carried her off to safety. *If only it could be true.*

Gena clutched her stomach and curled into a ball on the bed. It was then that she remembered the visit with her OB/GYN.

"Congratulations, you're going to have a baby."

A baby, my baby. She couldn't help but think of the unborn child she was carrying as she rubbed her stomach. She was in a dire predicament. *That's right, I was going to tell him about the baby,* she thought to herself, remembering how nervous she was and how she couldn't wait to hear what he would say. She had been hoping that Jerrell would be pleased with her and happy for the both of them. She was so ready to be with him and be a family. *How could I have been so dumb? He didn't love me, he didn't even care about me. He was trying to kill me.* Gena couldn't believe it. She was carrying the child of a man who had tried to kill her, fantasizing about a man who had been dead now for almost a year. *I can't believe Jerrell has me here. It's only a matter of time before he comes back to finish me off. My only chance will be to try and escape, go get my money, and get out of town. That's what Jerrell wanted, Quadir's money. He never wanted to be with me. He could have cared less.* That reality brought a tear to Gena and she realized at that moment that Jerrell had only been pretending to love and care about her. *How was I so stupid that I didn't see him for what he really was? I can't believe he was after my money.* Gena just sat on the edge of the bed thinking about everything that had happened, unable to justify anything and unwilling to believe that it was all happening to her. *I wonder where he is. Shit, where the hell am I? And how long have I been here?* She needed to get in touch with Gah Git. She needed to talk to her grandmother and tell her where she was and let her know that she was all right. Gah Git would be worried half to death. *Poor Gah Git, I hope she's okay.* Gena had already looked around the room and there was no phone. *Someone has to help me. I need to be rescued. But rescued from who? Whoever it is that bandaged my wounds, fed me, and took care of me? Yes, I definitely need to be rescued, especially if that person is Jerrell.*

The door to the room cracked open and Gena expected

the worst. Instead, she was greeted by a plump and friendly housekeeper.

"Oh, señorita, you're awake!" the housekeeper told her. "Oh, they will be so pleased! Mr. Smith is about to have breakfast on the porch. I can bring your breakfast out there so that you can dine with him. He will be so pleased, señorita! It is so good to see that you are awake now!"

"Mr. Smith? Who is Mr. Smith?" Gena asked.

"Why, that is Señorita Hopkins's boyfriend," Consuela explained. "Señor Smith is the one who rescued you and brought you here."

"Rescued me?" Gena was confused. She shook her head to rid herself of the cobwebs inside. *Who is Mr. Smith?* Gena needed to see this Mr. Smith. She needed to talk to him and she needed him to fill in all of the blanks from that night. *What had happened? Where was Jerrell? What was Mr. Smith doing there? Why did he bring her here?* She had a million and one questions that needed answering.

Gena threw the covers off of her legs and began to rise. Consuela rushed to her, and helped her stand.

"No, wait here," Consuela told her. "Señorita Hopkins brought something for you, just for when this day would come."

Consuela rushed out of the room, and returned seconds later with a metal walker. She placed the walker in front of Gena and then clasped Gena's arm.

"I'll help you to the elevator and then to the porch. I'll bring you breakfast out in the garden."

"Thank you so much," Gena told her. "You are very kind."

Consuela helped Gena to the elevator, where they rode it

to the first floor. The doors to the elevator opened, revealing a massive two-story family room. The dimensions made Gena gasp.

The room was forty by sixty, with a ten-foot-diameter wrought-iron chandelier. Antique furnishings and expensive décor filled the room. The art and tapestries that hung on the wall was all original, while the tables all looked to be hand-carved with great care and detail.

"Who lives here?" Gena asked.

"Señorita Hopkins," Consuela told her. "She is at work right now. Señor Smith is out on the lanai."

Gena followed as Consuela led her across the living room, out of the large double patio doors, and onto the lanai. A gentleman was seated across the lanai, facing away from them, looking over the swimming pool. She could see that he was dressed in all white, and reading a newspaper. A table with a pitcher of orange juice was next to him, and she could see that he had already poured a glass.

"Señor Smith," Consuela called out to him. "Look who has awakened."

Gena watched as the stranger rose from the chair and turned to her. Consuela had to catch her.

"Señorita, are you all right?" Consuela asked.

It can't be, it can't be. Gena shook her head.

"I'll take it from here," he told Consuela.